About the Book

Winner of the 1962 Carnegie Medal for the outstanding juvenile book by an English author

There were twelve of them—and they were all distinct personalities. Butter Crashey was the patriarch of the Twelves, and he was 140 years old. Crackey was only five, and Gravey was grave and melancholy. There was the Duke of Wellington, a most dignified fellow, and Stumps, whose history was "long, complicated and shrouded in mystery."

Max loved all twelve wooden soldiers, and he longed to share his secret about them. They were alive!

Max finally shares his secret with his sister and later with his older brother. They learn that historians are searching for the wooden soldiers that once belonged to the famous Brontë children. Could the Twelves be those same soldiers? And how can Max help them on their determined journey to their former home?

The Return of the Twelves is a wonderful story; full of humor and excitement, and that extra quality of imagination which makes this book so outstanding.

THE RETURN OF THE TWELVES

THE RETURN
OF THE
TWELVES

by Pauline Clarke

Illustrations by Bernarda Bryson

Coward-McCann, Inc.
New York

082012
First American Edition 1963
Text © 1962 by Pauline Clarke
Illustrations © 1963 by Coward-McCann

Library of Congress Catalog Card Number 63-15541

Manufactured in the United States of America

May the Four Genii forgive
us for playing with
their soldiers

CONTENTS

THE RETURN OF THE TWELVES

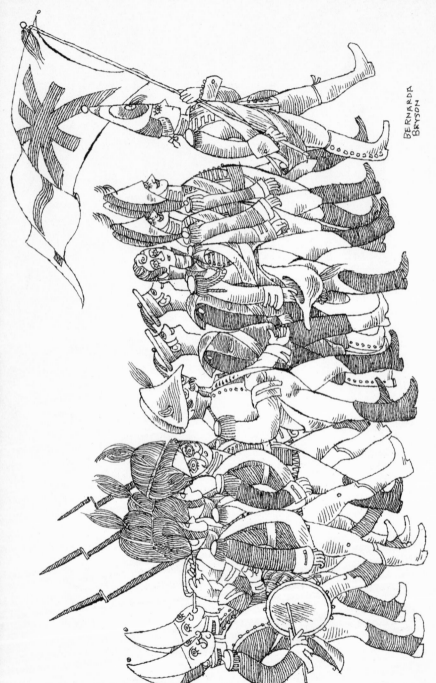

Tip tap tip tap tip tap stamp!

1

The Attic

MAX sat on the bare stairs below the attic, wondering whether to tell anyone.

His socks were down around his ankles. It had suddenly become too hot for socks, but it hadn't yet dawned on Max to take them off. His hands drummed tunes on the step beside him or played the harp down the wooden bannisters. At short intervals he put finger and thumb into his mouth, picked out his huge round candy ball, observed what color it was now and put it back. He kept frowning slightly, and when he wasn't making a noise with his hands, he listened. His rather large ears stuck out from his head as if listening made them larger.

There it was again.

Max stopped his loud sucking and gulped, in order to listen. His eyes were wide open, his eyebrows high up, and one cheek was swollen into a great bulge by the candy. He looked like a deformed, surprised dwarf.

Of course they would say it was rats.

Anyone would.

Or birds under the roof.

Pit pat tipper tapper scrabble stamp. Whee. Whish. Sizzle whizzle. That was the whispering.

He supposed that to them, that size, it was the proper way to speak. If you were that size and said something, that's what it would sound like. Even if you shouted like old Buster, the sergeant at school who taught physical training, it wouldn't sound loud. Max imagined, with great pleasure, old Buster shrinking to their size. How he would roar with terror. He would think he was going to vanish, and everyone would laugh. And his roar would gradually get quieter and whinier as he shrank.

Tip tap tip tap tip tap tip tap stamp.

This time it was so regular that only silly people

14

would think it was rats. They might think it was a robin breaking a snail shell or a woodpecker working at tree bark. Max knew it was none of these.

He knew quite well what it was, and in a minute he would get up, if he could without making a creak, and look at them. Should he call Jane, perhaps, while it was going on, and tell only her? Just Jane.

She would have to believe it if she saw it.

But if she made a noise, they might freeze (they *would*), and she would laugh at him and call him batty.

His heart felt big with such a thrilling secret inside it.

He didn't know how *not* to tell someone.

But of course, once he had told, then it would no longer be his secret. There would be the joy of telling, of showing Jane, of proving it, and then there would be Jane wanting to join in everything and enjoy it too. Also, it might be better to wait till they weren't frightened of him. They still were; they would still freeze if he went in. He longed to be real friends with them; he could think of the funniest things they could do, if only they would trust him and let him pick them up. Perhaps it would be better to get them to trust him first, before he told even Jane.

As stealthy as an animal, he stood, turned, knelt by the attic door and put one sparkling gray eye to the keyhole.

There they were. Three rows of four. Drilling.

It was funny to see them drilling so smartly in such shabby uniforms. There was scarcely any paint left. It must have been scarlet once. Perhaps if they trusted him, they would let him paint them. Give them a new coat of paint. Max grinned. This was exactly right.

Jane came to the landing below and saw Max kneeling at the attic door. He turned his head, one eye still screwed up and the other cheek as fat as a golf ball.

Jane shrieked with laughter. "Max, what *are* you doing? You look absolutely crazy," she said. "I didn't know this was where you said your prayers."

"Oh, shut *up*," Max hissed through one side of his mouth.

"What is it? One of your secret games? I know, you're just going to be beheaded! Who are you? Sir Walter Raleigh?"

Max stood up, made a face as best he could hindered by his candy, and remained silent.

"You can choke on those things, you know. We're all going to Bradford. You've got to come."

"Who says? Dirty old Bradford," he said, though Jane couldn't understand him.

"We've got to buy things. For the house. And Mummy says she's sick of getting furniture settled and she wants to spend some money. I don't blame her, do you?"

They had been here only a week, in this old farmhouse. They were all so glad to have moved to the country that they couldn't stop saying so.

"I'm going to stay here," Max said. (That's what he said, but Jane had to guess.)

16

"What? Please take that candy out."

"Maxy!" called Mrs. Morley. "Come on, quickly."

Max went to the next landing, leaned over the bannister, took out his candy and called to her.

"Mummy, may I please stay here? I have something entirely special I want to do."

When Max, who was eight, made speeches with long words, his mother couldn't refuse him. He had learned this and he used it when he needed to.

"You'll be sorry, you know. We'll be gone two or three hours. All of us. Daddy too," she said.

"I won't be sorry, I'll be glad," he answered.

"What about tea?"

"Aren't you even coming back for tea?"

"We *may* not. You may have a piece of cake and two buns. And bread if you want it. Be careful of the bread knife."

"Yes," he said.

"Good-bye, darling. Bill's around in the farmyard if you want him. Don't do stupid things, will you?"

"No," said Max. "I never do."

Jane jeered. So did Philip, who had joined them.

"Isn't he coming, our little man?" said Philip.

Max stuck his stained orange tongue out at Philip, popped his candy in again, and turned his back on them.

"What's he up to, Jane?"

"I don't know," she said. "When I came up, he was either saying his prayers or being beheaded outside the attic. I don't know which. Kneeling down."

"Both, I'll bet. Naturally," Philip said, "you'd say

17

your prayers if you were about to depart this life."

"He makes up so many things in his mind," said Mrs. Morley, "it might be anything."

2

The Patriarch

MAX waited until he heard the car doors slam and the engine purr and sing. Then he raced down to his own room and leaned out of the window in time to see the back of the station wagon disappear out of the driveway. For a minute he felt sorry and lonely.

He went quickly up the attic stairs and looked through the keyhole again.

The wooden soldiers stood exactly as he had seen them when Jane interrupted. They hadn't moved a tenth of an inch. They were as dead as ninepins. They had frozen again. Max sighed, enraged. It would be miserable if he had kept himself from going with the others for nothing.

All the same, he didn't give up hope. He had seen them move twice now, and what you saw you believed. (Like everyone else, Max also believed many things he didn't see.)

The candy ball was getting more manageable now,

and as he knelt there Max turned it over and over in his mouth. Suddenly he crunched it all up with determination and impatience. He decided to go in.

He wandered around the attic, pretending to be busy looking at things, but all the while keeping a cautious eye on them. It felt to him as though they were keeping cautious eyes on him too. It was like two cats casually looking away from each other, but each really wondering if the other was going to pounce.

Max felt as though he and his family had always lived in this house. He remembered the time they first came up here to the attic, carrying the stool, the boat and the drum.

Mrs. Morley had said, "Now, we won't banish Great-Grandpa's Ashanti things forever, but since I don't know quite where they're going, will you take them carefully up to the attic, please?"

Philip, Jane and Max were only too eager to explore the attic. Philip had seized the heavy carved wooden stool with its curved seat; Jane had clasped the curious-shaped, skin-covered drum to her chest; Max had taken the carved model canoe. Their great-grandfather had been a missionary on the Gold Coast of West Africa. He had gone up the Niger River farther than any other missionary before him, no doubt in just such a boat. He had talked to kings who thought it was quite all right to kill people for sacrifices. He had seen the pits where they threw them and huts that were full of skulls.

Now Max came to the stool, sat down on its curve—which fitted him so comfortably—and looked squarely at the soldiers. On just such a stool, their mother had often told them, the kings of Ashanti were crowned. She had been told by Grandma, who was the daughter of the missionary.

Max had stayed behind that first time, to explore thoroughly. He had stamped around the attic just as he had seen the contractor do, jumping on boards and tapping walls. He had been rewarded by finding the loose board near the window. Max never left things half explored. He got his knife, pried up the board, and found the dirty roll of torn rag in which the old soldiers were. Twelve of them.

"After all," said Max aloud, "I did rescue you from a living death."

He thought this was a fine expression; he had read it in a book lately. Although they were so old and battered, it was exciting and mysterious to find them hidden and to wonder who had hidden them. Added to this, when he brought them to show the family, his mother was quite impressed.

"Max, how interesting! Take care of them, because I should think they're really old. They ought to be in a museum."

"How old, Mummy? How old, Daddy?" Max asked, clutching the soldiers in his two hands.

"Careful! They look a bit frail," his father had said. He took one and scrutinized it. "Not much face left, or paint. He has a sort of high black cap on. I should think they're Napoleonic, or probably Wellington, being English, from what you can see of their clothes."

"Well, *how* old, Daddy?" Max persisted.

"Over a hundred years, if I'm right, Max. Take

care of them, please. I don't know that you should be allowed to play with them."

"But I found them!" Max exploded. And of course, because they were admired and valued, Max quickly became devoted to them. Jane said they were shabby, and Philip said they were worm-eaten (which wasn't true; it was only because he hadn't found them himself). But Max adored them. One or two still had a round flat stand with two holes in it for their feet. They weren't all the same size; some were taller than others. And although their faces were blurred and rubbed, you could still tell that each was different. Mrs. Morley said this was delightful because it proved they were handmade, each carved with his own face. Max agreed.

But all this was nothing compared to the time, two days ago, when Max had set them out on the attic floor, and lying on his tummy, had beat with his fingers on the Ashanti drum, so that they could march to it. Before his startled eyes, one of them, a tallish fellow—and at once noticed for his sly, birdlike alertness—hopped and twirled into life at the sound of the drum. He threw his tiny arms in the air, as if he were glad to feel life again. He skipped along the ranks, punching some in the jaw, tweaking the noses of others, and tripping the feet of the most stolid. Then once more he found his place in line, and all twelve stood to surprised attention and took at least ten tiny steps forward over the boards.

When Max half started to his feet in excitement, they stopped. They froze like a toad does when you meet him crossing the lawn. Even the lively fellow froze.

Then today, Max had heard their tiny noises and seen them at it. Before Jane had come and spoiled everything.

Now he knew he must be gentle and careful and not do sudden things. Max was a persistent boy and patient for his age (which isn't a patient age), so he just sat there on the Ashanti stool, with his hands on his thin knees, wondering if an Ashanti king had been crowned on it. Max could wait as long as they could. They would trust him sooner or later. Surely they knew he loved them?

If he were an Ashanti king, the first person he would sacrifice would be Anthony Gore. He knew that it was wrong to make human sacrifices, but then, if he were an Ashanti king in those old days, he *wouldn't* know this, so it would be all right. He supposed. When the Ashanti kings knew better, they stopped doing it. Max wondered if they missed it very much.

Max sighed and tried smiling at the soldiers. Then with two fingers he tapped out the rhythm of a song on the drum which stood beside him. He started to sing it, almost in a whisper, so as not to frighten them.

> "Oh, the brave old Duke of York,
>   He had ten thousand men;
>   He marched them up to the top of the hill,
>   And he marched them down again."

It was the only marching song he could think of about old soldiers.

"And when they were up, they were up,
And when they were down, they were down,
And when they were only halfway up,
They were neither up nor down."

Max piped it very quietly, soft as a pin. To his joy, the soldiers broke ranks and clustered together in a little band. Again he heard that faint crackling, whisking sound which was their talk. He wasn't surprised this time, because he'd been expecting it. He kept still.

One of them turned away from the others and came boldly across the attic floor to Max. Behind this one, prancing from side to side as if to urge him on, came the lively soldier Max had first seen move. The lively one finally gave the other a good push, but the first one seemed to be a stately and dignified character and he didn't lose his balance. Then they all bowed low from the waist, and the one in front lifted his arms and waggled his head.

Now, does he want me to pick him up? Max wondered. Did he dare? Would it frighten them?

He gently put out his hand, leaned down, and grasped the dignified little soldier by the waist. It was no bigger than that lizard he had picked up on the moor the other day. The fellow waved his arms, but didn't struggle.

Max brought him close up to his face. Perhaps the soldier wanted to say something. Max held him close to his ear. There was a crackle. Max closed his eyes and listened very hard, holding his breath. The crackle came again, in more of a pattern. Max brought the soldier a little nearer. The third time, he could hear and understand.

"Are you one of the Genii?" asked the creature.

Max had read *The Arabian Nights*, so he knew all about the Genii, those spirits who preside over a person's destiny all his life. If these soldiers wanted him to be a Genie to them, he didn't mind.

"Yes," he said, very solemnly and quietly. He was surprised to hear a sudden faint sprinkle of sound like rice falling on the floor. The soldiers were clapping.

"I am Butter Crashey," said the small fellow Max held. Max didn't know what to say to this. Should he say How do you do? Or I like you very much? Or How old are you? Or Where did you come from? None of these seemed quite right, and the last two seemed rude.

"I like your name," he said at last. "How did you get it?"

"I fell into the butter long ago," said his friend.

"I thought you must have," said Max.

"I am the patriarch of the Twelves," he went on, "and my age is one hundred and forty."

Max had a vague idea that if a person was very old, it was proper to congratulate him. "Good for you," he said. Then he thought this didn't sound old-fashioned enough, so he added, "Allow me to congratulate you upon being full of years and wisdom."

This was the way Philip spoke sometimes. Max felt pleased with it and so, it was clear, did Butter Crashey. He bent his head to acknowledge the compliment. Now that he was alive, his face had become sharp and detailed. It was no longer blurred and

25

featureless with being so old. It was like bringing a scene properly into focus through a pair of field glasses. Max looked at all the others and saw that the same was true of them. The jaunty soldier seemed to have particularly piercing eyes, and he made a face as Max looked. Max was delighted.

"Under your protection," announced Butter Crashey, "we propose to make a journey of discovery, as we once set forth under the four Genii to carve out a kingdom among the Ashanti."

"That's a very good idea," said Max, who was longing to see the soldiers moving around downstairs. He put the patriarch gently down with the others and went to the attic door. He opened it and stood to one side. The twelve soldiers formed into a column and marched toward the door and out onto the landing.

3

The Perilous Descent

WHEN they reached the fearful precipice of the stairs, they halted, broke out of their column, and stood along the top step like people on top of a cliff. They waved their arms, peered over, nudged one another, pointed, consulted each with his neighbor, and then gathered around one who was taller than the rest. Max had noticed him before. He was good-looking and well made and dashing. He might not be as old and wise as Butter Crashey or as impulsive as the lively one, but he looked more of a leader. Max wondered if he had a name, too, and what it was.

But he didn't want to interrupt their preparations.

They formed into a line again and lay down, every man holding onto the ankles of the one ahead. The first was the tall leader; the last was the patriarch.

But the leader was the other way around, holding the hands of the next and facing him. He wriggled to the edge of the top stair and began to drop carefully down, backwards. The steep attic stair was twice as tall as he was. Before he had touched ground, the man holding him was leaning well over but held safely by his ankles. The leader gave a small shout, let go of the man's hands, and jumped, sprawling onto the first stair.

Well done, Max said to himself as he saw the brave soldier recover his balance and stand squarely against the perpendicular wall of the stair.

The next man then turned around, held the hands of the one behind him, and was let over in the same way. But he landed on the shoulders of the waiting leader and then slipped down his back to the ground.

Max watched fascinated as each soldier in turn was lowered. But what was going to happen to Butter Crashey? As it was, he was having difficulty holding the last man without being tugged over. However, the patriarch, one hundred and forty though he was, turned around on his stomach, wriggled his legs over, and holding onto the top, lowered himself down. His legs waved. There was a shrill shrieking from the others. The jaunty soldier pranced with excitement. And then the patriarch found the shoulders of the tall leader. He was lifted down by the willing arms of all the rest.

But this was only one step. Now they clustered at the brink of the next. Max could see their difficulty. There wasn't room for them to lie in a column and

A perilous descent

BERNARDA
BRYSON

hold each other this time. What they needed was a rope or a ladder.

We'll be here all night, he said to himself, thinking.

His instinct told him that if he were to pick them all up, put them into the shoe box where he kept them, and carry them down, they might think it a terrible insult. They might freeze again at once, to pay him back. What he had to do was to think up some better way and let them discover it.

He went into the attic and got the ball of string which was kept in a trunk full of brown paper for packages. He tied one end firmly to the bannister post, low down, so that if a soldier stood on the slope the wooden spindles were fitted into, he could hold onto the string and walk down the slope as if it were a ramp. Then Max crept past the chattering soldiers, down the stairs with the string, now and then putting it around a spindle to keep it firm. Around the corner he went and down to the next landing, making two turns of string at the big posts and so on until he had made a handrail down the two main flights to the hall. Then he pulled the string firm, tied a good knot, and cut it off the ball. All they had to do was to climb up onto the slope. Surely they could help each other up; they seemed sensible and agile.

To his utter delight, he met the tall leader on the first landing, waiting at the foot of the slope as if he were taking the salute at a review. Above him at different intervals came the others. One ran down shouting a thin war cry. The next slid sideways, both hands on the rope and facing it. The third was sitting down as if he were on a sledge, his hand holding the rope above him. One came down backwards. The lively one used the rope as a trapeze and swung with his feet drawn up, screaming a thin scream of glee. Max was enchanted. They were all different, like real people. He was only sorry he had missed seeing them discover their rope. He looked up in time to see the venerable Butter Crashey heave the last man up to the ramp. But before the last man descended, he turned around, and holding the string to steady himself, held out a hand to the patriarch and pulled him aloft.

"Hooray!" Max couldn't help shouting. "You're all different. You're sensible. You think of each other too."

The patriarch marched solemnly down the slope, as befitted one so old, slow and upright. This he somewhat spoiled by slipping on the last lap and landing on his back with his heels in the air. But the others respected him so much that none laughed (except Max) and all quickly gathered to pick him up.

The delight of the Twelves, as the patriarch had called them, in finding that the rope went on all the way down was lovely to see. Max rubbed his hands (very softly) with pleasure. They made the descent more and more quickly, with shouts of glee and abandon the faster they went, so that they sounded like a miniature flock of whistling, calling, twittering birds in a woods after rain.

Now what would they do? All the doors stood open. They could turn into the dining room or the living room or the study. They could march along to the kitchen. They could even sniff the open air from the front door which stood wide, and go out into the sunlight.

At this minute the hot afternoon stillness was shattered by the piercing ring of the telephone. As he hurried to answer it Max couldn't help watching the soldiers. They jumped as if they were shot, and clustered together, holding their hands to their ears and looking up into the sky. (Or the ceiling.)

Max reached the telephone, seized it, and stopped its ringing.

"Hullo," he said. He hadn't learned his new number yet, and he was too startled to say anything else. He kept his eye on the soldiers.

"Maxy?"

"Yes?"

"Are you all right, darling?"

"Yes, perfectly."

"What are you doing?"

"Oh, fooling around."

"You were right near the phone."

"Yes, I'm in the hall."

The Twelves had lined up and were heading for the living room.

"In the hall? Why don't you play in the garden?"

This was the kind of silly question grownups always asked.

"Because I like being in the hall," Max said patiently. "Anyway, I'm going into the living room now."

They had disappeared into the living room. He was missing all the fun, yet it was nice of his mother to call him up.

"Have you had your tea?"

"Not *yet*. I haven't had time," Max said.

"When you have it, you may give Brutus his milk."

"Where *is* Brutus?" Max asked, a sudden horrible thought striking him.

"Last seen by me in the green chair in the living room," said his mother.

"Help! Well, good-bye, Mummy. I'm in the middle of something."

"Good-bye, darling. Glad you're all right."

Max slammed the receiver down and hurried to the living room. The soldiers were marching over the carpet unsuspectingly, letting out little sounds of amazement.

Brutus, wakened by the telephone, had reared up in his chair and was stretching, his back arched like a croquet hoop, the fur on his fat legs parting in flakes. Hearing Max, he turned around and saw them moving.

His ears went pointed, his whiskers were pushed forward, his mouth opened slightly, and he yickered as he did when he saw a bird near by.

"Brutus!" Max gasped. Brutus took a flying leap and landed smack on top of the moving soldiers.

"Oh, help! Help!" Max said, diving forward. "You've squashed them. You'll kill them, you awful cat." He seized Brutus and lifted him up. The soldiers, winded and terrified, fled in all directions; all except one limp form clutched in the crook of Brutus' great white paw. Max gently detached him, put Brutus out, and shut the door. The poor little fellow was in a complete swoon, and no wonder. Max laid him on the carpet and waited. Soon the noble Butter Crashey came out from under a chair, and the others followed cautiously.

They ran to their companion and began to cheer him up. They lifted his head and rubbed his hands.

"Take heart, Bravey. Remember your own saying, 'Eat, drink and be merry, for tomorrow we die.' But you aren't dead, I assure you."

"The Genii have protected you."

"Pray sit up and stop fainting," said the jaunty soldier crossly, jealous of the attention the sufferer was getting.

"Give him air."

"Let Cheeky get at him! Let the stouthearted doctor see him. Out of the way, Monkey."

"Stand back, Crackey and Tracky," said one, who must have been the doctor.

Max saw the doctor make a few movements over the soldier called Bravey, feel his pulse, and rub his hands. Bravey came to, blinked, and sat up.

"Quite resuscitated," said Cheeky the doctor.

"Made alive," added the patriarch.

"Bring him some wine," suggested the tall leader.

"It little becomes the Duke to ask for wine in the wilderness," said one. Max crossed to the cupboard where his father kept the drinks. He took out the tiniest glass there, meant for liqueurs, poured a drop of sherry into it, and brought it over to the soldiers.

"The Genii can do anything," he said softly, "even bring wine in the desert."

They gathered around the glass with whoops of joy.

34

They dipped Bravey's finger in and made him suck it. At once he became more cheerful and talkative.

"Eat, drink and be merry," he squealed.

Soon they were all dipping their hands in and sucking, and the noise was considerable.

4

The Duke of Wellington

THE sherry was certainly putting heart into the Twelves. The more they sucked, the more noisy they became, and some began to shake their fists as if they meant battle. Max swooped down his finger and thumb, silently took the glass away, and returned it to the cupboard. They looked for it for awhile, but soon gave up and began to explore again. As they were so very brave and gay at the moment, Max decided to risk picking one up. He choose the tall leader whom somebody had called the Duke. The Duke looked a little amazed at feeling himself clutched and flying through the air, but he didn't stiffen. He felt wriggly and lively as a lizard. Max put him down on the open piano.

"If Your Grace likes to march along here," he said

softly, "it will be as good as a band." His Grace stepped onto a slippery white key which gradually let him down as it thundered out a deep note. Feeling himself going down, he held out his arms to keep his balance, and strode quickly on up the scale from note to note, filling the living room with a tinkle of music.

This seemed to excite the others even more. Butter Crashey had led a small party toward the French window where they were looking out on the garden, their hands against the glass. The one called Monkey had climbed up onto a pile of books waiting to be put away, reached the swinging curtain cord, and was now swarming up it like a sailor. After him went the two called Crackey and Tracky, as if the cord were the rigging of a ship. The cord swung as they climbed.

Meanwhile, poor Bravey, overcome first by Brutus and then by the sherry, had stumbled as far as the white fur rug by the fireplace and was marching bravely over it like a man through a snowdrift, sinking up to his knees and often falling flat on his face. As he scrambled up he was still saying, "Give us good cheer, eat, drink, dance and be merry," though his voice was certainly a little thick.

Max kept his eye on them all in turn, for he didn't want to lose any. The Duke had reached the top of the scale and was now skating back, making an exciting trill as he lightly skimmed over the notes.

Max decided that he was hungry and saw that it was teatime. First shutting the soldiers carefully into the living room, he went out to the kitchen, took Brutus from the window sill, and gave him his milk outside the back door. Then he got the cake and the

37

The daring midshipmen

BERNARDA
BRYSON

buns and the bread, the butter and jam, a large glass of milk and everything else he needed, and put them on the kitchen table.

Now. He went back to the living room. He didn't want to pick everyone up without any warning, in case it frightened them and spoiled their fun. Added to this, the most interesting part of the affair was to see what they could arrange on their own.

He went over to Butter Crashey, who, with his few followers, was now watching the antics of Monkey, Crackey and Tracky on the curtain cord. The cord was swinging wildly. Monkey wanted to slide down, Tracky wanted to get to the top, and Crackey was caught in the middle. Monkey kicked him from above; Tracky butted him from below. The patriarch's men were standing at the bottom of the cord, urging on their favorites, and the noise was like a cat fight.

The patriarch was trying to stop the quarrel and calm the fighters by holding his arms up, clapping slowly, and saying, "Hush! Halt! Have done!"

Max lifted up Crashey, still giving orders, and whispered, "I want you all to come into the kitchen. How can we collect everyone?"

The patriarch looked at him a moment with his mouth open and then replied, "Without doubt, the Duke must blow his trumpet. This is what he always did when he was a humble trumpeter, and the Twelves obeyed. Tell him to do this, and see what follows."

"But he hasn't got a trumpet," Max said.

"No, he has become too grand since he was a duke," said the patriarch.

"What is he duke of?" asked Max.

"He is Arthur Wellesley, Duke of Wellington," said Butter Crashey solemnly, "which honor came to him after the famous Battle of Waterloo. But perhaps you don't know about Waterloo?"

"I know all about Waterloo," Max said. "I'll tell him to tootle without a trumpet."

Still carrying Crashey, he went over to the piano.

"The patriarch commands Your Grace to collect the Twelves," explained Max.

The Duke stopped dead on middle C and lifted his empty hands in despair. However, the tootle he produced from his own small throat was bold, piercing and commanding (it reminded Max of a bird's whistle), and before he had finished, Max saw the soldiers gathering.

Max put the patriarch on the carpet, lifted down the Duke of Wellington, and helped Bravey out of his jungle. Tracky slid down the curtain cord, followed quickly by the others, and soon the whole band was marshaled behind the Duke and marching toward the kitchen.

Max lifted them gingerly onto the kitchen table one by one and was pleased to see that they didn't seem to mind. Then he sat down to enjoy his tea and watch what they would do.

They marched all around the kitchen table as if to make sure where they were. Then they came nearer to Max's end and walked around the breadboard, pointing up at the loaf as if it were a small hill. They

The feast at Sandwich

showed great interest in the butter too; all the more when Max cut a piece off and put it on his plate.

Then they gathered around his plate, sat in a circle, and watched each mouthful he took.

"Like Brutus," Max said. "I'll bet you're hungry."

He gave each man a large crumb of bread followed by a smaller crumb of cake, and they ate with relish.

"Tell me about your famous expedition to carve out your kingdom among the Ashanti," Max said. "I know it's ignorant of me not to have heard of it," he added, "but I'm only eight."

"Crackey is only five," remarked a grave-looking soldier whom Max hadn't noticed before, "and *he* has heard of it."

"Of course he's heard of it, if he went on it," argued Max rather rudely. The whole lot threw back their heads and laughed at the grave soldier, who looked more sour than ever. The jaunty one even pointed and jeered.

"You are answered, Gravey," said the Duke.

"Why is he called Gravey?" Max asked. "Did he fall in the gravy or is it to rhyme with Bravey?"

"Both," said several soldiers thoughtlessly.

"Neither," said Butter Crashey. "He is grave and melancholy, so his name is naturally Gravey."

"I say, Gravey," Max began, seeing the poor fellow scowling and drawing his brows together. "I *am* sorry I answered you back. Please tell me about the expedition."

The soldiers began to twitter, and those next to the patriarch nudged him with their elbows.

42

The patriarch swallowed his last crumb of cake, cleared his throat, and began to speak.

"We set out in a ship called the *Invincible*," he said. "I was the captain, Cheeky was the surgeon and the most stouthearted man in the ship. The rest were trumpeters and sailors, and those fellows you saw climbing the rope were midshipmen. After many adventures, including storms and battles with enemies, we reached Africa, fought the Ashanti, and began to build our first town."

At this minute there was a loud engine noise in the yard, the doors of a car slammed, footsteps ran toward the house, voices yelled and called, and the back door—which Max had carefully closed to keep Brutus out—was flung open with a whoop by Jane.

The effect of all this noise was horrifying. The Twelves scattered in all directions. Several ran to the edge of the table and fell hurtling to the ground. The lively one bumped against the breadboard and went flat on his face at the foot of bread hill, lying as if he were stunned. Some simply swooned where they were and slumped as if dead. The patriarch stumbled over the butter dish, fell head first, and was caught by his head and fists in the soft mound.

"Here he is! Here he is!" Jane shrieked.

Max, scarlet with rage and fright, dived under the table to rescue the fallen. There was no time to be polite or gentle. He snatched them up, counting as he went. One had crawled toward the stove, and Jane's foot was nearly on him.

"Look *out*!" Max yelled.

"All right," she said crossly. "What is it? What's the matter?"

"Eight, nine," muttered Max, standing up, his hair over his eyes. "Ten," he said, seizing the greasy Butter Crashey. "Eleven," he added, tenderly rescuing the little soldier on the breadboard.

"*Eleven*," said Max, worried.

"Eleven what? What are you doing? Oh, those dirty old soldiers."

"Shut up," said Max.

"Don't be so cross, Maxy dear. Here we all are. What is it?"

"You're back much earlier than you said." Max scowled.

"We didn't say," Mr. Morley said. "Let's have some tea."

"Yes, come on. Move over, Max, and we'll set the table," said his mother, dumping her packages.

"Our little man seems upset," Philip remarked. "I'm ravenous," he said, taking a bun.

"I've had my tea," Max said with dignity, clutching his soldiers to his chest, "and there's one of the Twelves missing, so please don't step on him. *Please.* He's here somewhere."

"The twelves?" Mrs. Morley said, putting the kettle on. "What is the twelves?"

"The soldiers. The old soldiers."

"Oh, we'll find it and rescue it, darling."

"I don't know where he's gone."

"You've put him down somewhere. He hasn't *gone.*"

"He *has* gone," said Max stubbornly. He turned

44

and went out of the kitchen and tramped slowly up the stairs.

He could feel what had happened. They were all stiff and wooden in his hands; they were frozen. He laid them in their box, and their faces were blurred and old again.

"Oh, do come back soon. Don't freeze forever. Please, please don't. I want to hear about the expedition," Max whispered.

5

The Brontyfan

WHERE he had gone was a mystery, that missing soldier. Max spent all the next morning hunting. He had looked so thoroughly, in the kitchen and the pantry and the cabinets, that he had made his mother suspicious.

"But, Max, you didn't *play* in the pantry or the cabinets, did you? How could it have got there?"

It was no good saying that the fellow had walked. But this was the fact: he could have walked, unless he were wounded or dead from his fall. And in this case Max would have found him on the floor.

"Well, I went in to get my tea. My cake and bread and things," Max said slyly.

"Oh, I see. Did you go into the garden?"

"No."

"Because I don't think it's in here. Mrs. Hodgson has cleaned this room. She could have found it."

"Mummy, she couldn't have thrown him away? In

the trash or *on the fire*? Could she?" Max said suddenly, with horror.

"You can look in the trash. But I don't think she would. She'd see it was a soldier. I'll mention it to her. And, Maxy, while I think of it, must we have that piece of string tied all down the bannisters?"

"Yes, I need it monstrously," Max said, using a word of Philip's.

His mother laughed.

"What for, darling? It looks awful. And how can Mrs. Hodgson polish?"

"It's an important game. I can't keep taking it off. Anyway, she doesn't polish that slope the spindles are in."

"Indeed she does, I hope!"

"Well, I hope she doesn't. It'll make it so slippery."

"But nobody walks on the slope!"

"Oh, don't they?" Max muttered.

"What? You're not to play tricks with the bannisters, Max. You're certainly not to climb down outside; there's too far to fall."

"I wasn't going to."

"Philip tried it once at the other house."

"Did he?" Max said with interest. "I didn't know."

"Max," said his father, coming in from the living room, where he had been giving the parson some sherry. "Will you tell me what you've been doing with the sherry?"

"Why nothing, I—"

"What's this, then?" Mr. Morley held up the little liqueur glass with sherry in the bottom.

"Oh yes. I borrowed a little," Max said, grinning.

47

"Max! Did you drink it?" asked his mother.

"No, I didn't. It was just a game," Max said.

"You can play games with water. And not the best glasses," said his father.

"No, I needed sherry. Monstrously," Max said as he slipped out of the kitchen.

"He's lost that old soldier, Roderick. Will you look for it?" asked Mrs. Morley.

"I said he shouldn't be allowed to play with them. They should be in the living-room cabinet," said her husband.

"That seems so useless, doesn't it? He adores them."

"By the way, this parson's an absolute Brontë fan. Are you coming in?"

"Yes, in half a minute. Of course we're next door now, aren't we?" she replied as her husband hurried out. Max came back, his small dwarf face looking puzzled.

"What's a brontyfan?" he asked.

"I'll tell you later, darling. I must go and say how do you do to the parson," said his mother.

Brontyfan, Max muttered, walking up the stairs toward the attic. He might as well go and see. Once more. His heart was heavy, because it was two days. Was it perhaps because one was lost? Were they hurt in their feelings that he, the Genie, hadn't protected the twelfth? Brontyfan. It couldn't be that enormous prehistoric creature in the museum, although that was a bronty something, he knew. But no parson could be one of those. Unless his father meant he looked like it? Perhaps he had a huge, long neck?

48

Brontyfan. And also, what were they next door to? It sounded as if they were next door to its lair.

Max could hear Philip singing, exercising his funny cracking voice, he supposed. Philip was roaring:

"Brave Benbow lost his legs, by chain-shot, by chain-sho-o-t
Brave Benbow lost his legs, by chain-shot,
Brave Benbow lost his legs, and all on his stumps he begs,
Fight on my English lads, 'tis our lot, 'tis our lot."

Then Max heard the drum. *Ti tum tiddle um tum tum. Tum ti tum tum ti tum.* Philip was beating the Ashanti drum! Max flew up the last flight. He had suddenly remembered what happened when he last beat the drum! Why had he forgotten to try this? It was natural, after all, since they had once been on this expedition to Africa and fought the Ashanti, that his great-grandfather's drum should make them excited.

Philip sang on:

"Let a cradle now in haste on the quarter-deck be placed
That the enemy I may face till I die, till I die."

He finished with an absolute tattoo on the drum.

The attic door was open. Max stood there, breathing gustily and gazing at Philip, and then furtively looked toward the corner of the attic. The far corner. Where they all were. He had arranged them hopefully, in rows. They were moving.

He looked away quickly.

"What's up with you?" Philip said. "Seen a ghost?"

Max stepped between Philip and the soldiers. He didn't want to lose his secret. Not yet.

"Why are you playing the drum?" Max asked.

"Why shouldn't I? You haven't got a monopoly on this drum," said his brother.

"Listen, Phil," Max began hastily, "what's a brontyfan?"

Philip was silent a moment and then roared with laughter.

"Don't you know?" he teased.

Max's only thought was to get him out of the attic. He didn't care about this stupid brontyfan; it could be what it liked.

"What do you *think* it is?" Philip went on teasing him.

"Well, this parson's one, or like one I suppose, and he's in the living room and I think they want you to go down so you can say how do you do. Quickly! You might get some sherry," Max said, adding this as a bait.

"You come too," said Philip, bounding up from the Ashanti stool, "and we'll have a nice joke about Brontë fans. Come on, Maxy."

"No, I'm busy," Max said, tugging his sleeve away from Philip.

"Coward," said his brother, thundering down the stairs.

Max breathed again and shut the attic door. Then he crept to the stool and sat down. They hadn't moved far. They were coming. Max's pointed face spread into a slow smile. Butter Crashey, the Duke of Wellington and then a gap; on they came, in four rows of three this time. Gravey, Bravey and Cheeky; then the three whose names Max hadn't learned yet, one of them the fellow who had roused all the others the first time. Last came the wild young midshipmen who had climbed the curtain cord—Monkey, Tracky and Crackey. The gap was the missing soldier. Max could hardly bear to look at it. They halted, and the patriarch moved out. He went along the rows solemnly, pointing at each man. He pointed at himself last and scratched his head. Then the Duke did the same. A great burst of chattering arose as they broke ranks.

"Oh, they're counting," Max said. It was clear they had just realized there was a man short. Then they gathered in a band and all began saying the same thing. Louder and louder came the chant, until Max was able to hear what it was, even from his end of the attic. They droned:

> "Frederic Guelph, Duke of York!
> Frederic the first, King of the Twelves!
> After that, became Frederic the Second!
> Otherwise known to us as Stumps!
> Stumps! Stumps! Where is Stumps?"

Now I know who's lost, Max said to himself. His nickname is Stumps.

Butter Crashey left the group of chanting soldiers and came toward Max, who bent down and picked him up gently.

"I have come to consult you, Oh Genie," Butter Crashey began, "because Stumps is lost again."

"Oh, has he been lost before?" Max asked.

"Yes, indeed. He was lost upon Ascension Island on the way to Africa. He was killed by the enemy. When the others searched for him, to make him alive again, he had disappeared."

Max was glad to hear that they could make each other alive. This was splendid. No wonder they lasted so many years.

"And what was his real name?" he asked the patriarch, thinking of the chant he had just heard.

"The history of Stumps is long, complicated and shrouded in mystery," Butter Crashey said. "He was two people, and only the Genii know why; they decreed it. As Stumps, he was lost on the way to Africa. But he was also Frederic Guelph, Duke of York."

Max was pleased that there really was a Duke of York among them and he began to sing his song:

> "Oh, the brave old Duke of York,
> He had ten thousand men;
> He marched them up to the top of the hill,
> And he marched them down again."

The patriarch was evidently delighted with this compliment. He was balanced on Max's left hand, and he tramped up and down Max's arm as the boy sang, as if he were climbing a hill and coming down again. He felt like a sparrow on Max's bare skin.

"Go on about the Duke of York," Max said.

"As to the Duke of York, he was elected King of the Young Men and became Frederic the First."

"Who were the Young Men?" Max asked.

"Why, we are the Young Men," Butter replied, drawing himself up.

Max didn't like to remind him that he was one hundred and forty, so he simply said, "I thought you said you were called the Twelves."

"We are called both."

"Why?" asked Max.

Butter Crashey thought a moment. "It is a sign of low birth and no spirit to have but one name," he said. "You yourself are sometimes the Genie, sometimes Max."

Max smiled. "I didn't know you knew I was Max," he said.

"I have heard the name in the air," said the patriarch, waving his thin little arm.

"Well, go on about Frederic the First."

"Alas, he was killed in the first battle with the Ashantis. He was killed so dead that he couldn't be got alive. He was the best monarch that ever sat upon the throne of the Twelves." Butter sighed.

"If he was killed so dead that he couldn't be got alive," Max said, puzzled, "why is he still here? Because he was, until he got lost again."

"Ah, but I have told you. He was two people," the patriarch answered. "He was Stumps, remember, as well as the Duke. One day I heard a hollow, tomblike voice calling 'Crashey! Crashey!' I went out and returned with a ghastly skeletonlike figure clothed in tarnished regimentals. It was poor Stumps, come back from Ascension Island."

What marvelous stories he tells, thought Max. Aloud, he said, "I see." He saw perfectly well.

A noble gesture

This was absolutely what happened with soldiers. They did change names. They died, were made alive, got lost, turned up again and became someone else.

"Whereupon," said B. Crashey solemnly, "I said, 'Young Men, elect him for your king. All know his courage, coolness, integrity and ability.' So they did. He became Frederic the Second. He was a good king.

54

Though his qualities weren't shining, they were of sterling worth."

"But isn't he still king? What happened next?" Max asked. The Twelves seemed to have a complete history, like any other people.

"The last act of his reign was the best," said Butter Crashey. "When the Duke of Wellington, scourge of Napoleon, returned to Ashanti from the Battle of Waterloo and told us all his brave deeds, Frederic the Second arose and took the crown off his head and placed it on that of the Duke of Wellington, saying, 'I am not worthy to rule this man. He is your king.'" The patriarch held up his arms and removed an imaginery crown.

No wonder, thought Max, that the Duke is now the leader. He couldn't help feeling sorry for Stumps, thus demoted from being king. But, again, this was just what happened with soldiers; favorites were made and then they fell.

As if in answer to his thought, the patriarch nodded wisely. "If you want my opinion," he said, "he preferred being Stumps to being king. He was free and he liked adventures. So it isn't altogether surprising that he's lost again," he went on. "But if you will tell me, as an oracle, where to look, I will send out a search party."

Max frowned and considered. He didn't know where Stumps was. But as Genie, he didn't like to say so. It wouldn't do for Butter Crashey, who said he was their oracle—which Max thought meant a kind of prophet—to go back to the Twelves and say the Genie didn't know. Anyway, Max knew the rules of this game. What the Genii didn't know or hadn't considered, they must make up. He must even find another soldier if Stumps was gone forever.

"I myself am searching for your king," he said gravely. "If he doesn't return, consult me again." And with this oracular remark, Butter seemed satisfied.

6

Stumps

"WHO were you talking to?" Jane asked, standing outside the attic door. Max thought he had heard someone, but Jane was so light she crept about like a small wind, or it might be the wood of the old stairs creaking for no reason. Then there had been a little shuffle. He had quickly put the patriarch down with the others and gone to the attic door. Jane looked sheepish and she was smiling.

Max came out, shutting the door behind him. "You shouldn't have been listening," he said.

"It sounded interesting. Was it your game with your soldiers? Maxy, I wish you'd let me play. I like your games."

Max looked at Jane, considering. It was perfectly true that he and she had often made up wonderful games that went on for days. Jane was a good maker-up of games and she didn't let secrets out, usually. But lately she had played much less with Max and spent more time reading by herself. Max had thought she was getting too old to like made-up games, just as Philip had.

Jane had eyes the color of bluebells and now they were fixed on Max, trying to understand the look on his face. Her features were pale and pointed, rather like Max's, but what looked all right on a boy wasn't pretty enough for a girl. Jane's one beauty was her eyes.

"I like the weeny voice you use for them to answer in," she said. "I could hardly hear it, it sounded so whispery, but it went on quite a long time. How do you do it without moving your lips?"

"How do you know I don't move my lips? Jane, you're an eavesdropper *and* an eyedropper. You must have looked through the keyhole."

Jane laughed a high laugh which was like her mother's. "There's no such word as an eyedropper," she said.

"There is if I say so," said Max. "Anyway, you must have been," he accused her.

"Yes, I was. I couldn't hear the words very well, except something about searching, so I bet it's that soldier you've lost. Come on, Max, you've got to shake hands with the parson."

"That old brontyfan." Max scowled.

"How did you know he was a Brontë fan?"

"Heard Daddy say so. What does it mean, by the way?" Max asked, as casually as he knew how and as if he didn't care at all. This, he had learned, was the only way to find out things and at the same time not lose face. It might work with Jane, though older people like Philip always saw through it. Grownups saw through it, too, but they kindly pretended they hadn't, and explained.

"It's someone who's mad for the Brontës. You know, fan like in fan mail. For instance," Jane went on kindly as they marched downstairs side by side, Max hanging onto her waist, "if you're stuck on a movie star, then you're a fan of his."

But this wasn't Max's main problem. He knew about fans, now that he knew it was a separate word.

"But what *are* bronties?" he asked, hoping that Jane would go on being kind and not laugh.

"*The* Brontës. It's a family. They lived at Haworth. You know, it's quite near. And they were all so famous that it's a museum, the house they lived in. This parson has been telling us about it."

"What were they famous at?"

"They all wrote books. *Jane Eyre*'s the best book I've ever read," Jane said in the deep and glowing tone which her shrill voice took on when she was moved. "I've just finished it."

"Oh, is that the one with that mad woman shut up in it?" Max asked with interest. He had heard Jane talking about it.

"Yes. Surely you knew it was by Charlotte Brontë?"

"No, I didn't. What's this parson like?"

"All right. Nice."

Max liked him at once because he was perfectly serious.

"How do you do, Max. I'm interested to hear about the soldiers that you found," he said, shaking hands.

59

"Who told you?" Max asked, shaking the parson's hand firmly in return.

"Your mother."

"I've lost one, but he'll come back," Max said.

"I'm sure he will. May I see them sometime?"

Max gazed at him. The parson was still perfectly serious; he wasn't being patronizing.

"Maxy, Mr. Howson is very interested in old things and knows a lot about them."

"Butter's a hundred and forty," Max said, without thinking.

"What, darling?"

"When I've found the lost one, you could. Perhaps," Max said quickly to Mr. Howson.

"Thank you. Very much. I'll remember."

Max grinned at Mr. Howson, his wide mouth like a crescent moon above his pointed chin. He was imagining Mr. Howson's face if he saw the soldiers move. Mr. Howson grinned back. He was about forty-five, and he was tall and square-faced and black-browed and slightly tortured-looking when he didn't smile. Waving at them all, he drove away.

"I know, he's like Mr. Rochester!" Jane said at lunch. "Mr. Howson."

"Yes, he is, a little," her mother said.

"I *adore* Mr. Rochester," said Jane.

"Oh, Jane," Philip said, wriggling sentimentally and making a face.

"Who's Mr. Rochester?" Max asked.

"In *Jane Eyre*," said Jane.

"Pooh, these old Brontës," Max said, with dignity.

"Oh, so you've found out," Phil said. "You know

what, Mummy? He thought Mr. Howson was a kind of animal like a brontysaurus. Because of Brontë fan. Didn't you, Max? Admit it!"

How did Philip know? How did he know so exactly? It was absolute mind reading. Max scowled and then giggled, filling his mouth with potato.

But where was Stumps? Max lay in bed that night wondering. He had made another search in the afternoon. He had even gone around the yard and the garden with no success. When his mother lost something, she always went very carefully over what could have happened. Max lay watching the creeper leaves which framed his window. They were rustly and green. It wasn't dark yet, and the window was a square of pale green light, like water.

What would Stumps have done after finding himself in the kitchen? What could he have done? Max wondered, following his mother's example. He must think of all the things Stumps could have done. First he must have crawled quickly away somewhere to hide. It must have been a very good place, for neither Max nor Mrs. Hodgson to find him. He might have moved around while she cleaned, keeping out of her way.

Then what would he try to do? He was a valiant and sensible soldier, according to Butter Crashey, and used to adventures. He would certainly try to climb back to the attic to join the others. He wouldn't forget their exciting descent. He would wait until the kitchen door was left open and no huge and frightening people were around. Surely this was what he would do. This meant he would have to wait till nighttime.

But at night the kitchen door was never left open, because of Brutus. Stumps would come out to reconnoiter and find himself shut in. Max thought of Stumps going around, trying to find a way out of the kitchen and into the hall. Around and around he would go, feeling and peering and tapping and grumbling. He would probably spend the whole night that way. No window would be open, even if he could climb that high.

Now Max seemed to see him, as if he were really in the kitchen, watching. Stump's small arms were held up, exploring the kitchen walls, looking for holes, like a prisoner in a cell. He reached the crack where the door was, but it was tight shut. He came to the big, white hot-water heater, went around behind it, and came out the other side. Next to it was the stove, and all along below the window there were built-in cupboards. They were no good to Stumps. Around the corner again, to where the sink was. Stumps pushed in back of the plastic curtains that hung below the sink, and his heart beat because he thought he was getting out. But no, his hopes were dashed; there was a solid wall at the back. Then he came to the refrigerator and explored around it. Here was another door, and he could smell a slight smell of fresh air beyond it, but it was shut. It wasn't dark; the windowpanes were light. First they were light with moonlight. But later, as Stumps sat down, worn out with his wandering, he saw them grow light with daylight. He tried to climb the table leg, but fell back

62

exhausted. He tried to swarm up the plastic curtain, but it was so slippery he couldn't hold on. He sat below the sink, and had he not been Frederic, both the first and the second King of the Twelves, he would have cried. He found that by climbing on a great brush and a pile of soap-powder packages he could just reach the bend in the pipe below the sink. He heaved himself up, and wedged safely in the bend, he fell asleep.

No wonder I didn't find him, thought Max. And the next night Stumps would try again. Max didn't know whether he was dreaming or imagining now. The next night Stumps had better luck. The door into the pantry was open a crack, and beyond this, as he stumbled along over the tiles, he saw moonlight. He came at last to a little door only about three times his size, curved in a noble arch above his head. It was a strange door, because it didn't open right to the ground but seemed to be cut in the wall, more like a window. It was Brutus' cat door through which he ran in and out. Stumps heaved himself up and over and dropped down into the outside world! He was in the yard, but he was no nearer to the stairs and the long climb up to the attic. It seemed that he was farther away. He looked about him, bewildered in the bright light of the moon. He began to walk across the yard slowly.

Max felt the full moon shining on him, opened his eyes, and remembered all he had seen or dreamed or imagined about Stumps. Stumps! By now Stumps was making his way over the yard. Max leaped out of bed as if he were sure of this, and looked out of his window.

How diamond bright the moon was! It looked cold, it was so bright. But the summer night wasn't cold, only slightly chilly. The moon cast shadows as dark as charcoal. Each cobble of the path to the farmyard had a light side and a black side. The nasturtiums around the water barrel and the creeper leaves below Max's window threw dark stencils on the flagstones. It was so strange to see the bright middle of a moonlight night for almost the first time, as Max was doing, that for a minute or two he forgot *why* he was looking. He looked all around the yard, at the garage and the old stable and the sheds, and beyond to the pigpens. He would never forget what he saw and the sounds and smells that went with it.

Something moved in the middle of the yard—a small creature casting a small shadow. If it were a mouse, the shadow wouldn't be so thin. It must be Stumps. This was no more than Max had expected. The tiny figure had stopped now, and Max found it difficult to keep his eye on him, he was so small in the distance. What would he be doing? He would be looking up at the house, seeing how he could climb in, perhaps. This was what Max would do if he were shut out.

Then Max noticed for the first time that the great creeper that went past his window went on up to the attic. If Stumps were to climb it, he would be all right. But if the moon made him mad for wandering and he took it into his head to go exploring the pigpen, Max might never find him again.

BERNARDA
BRYSON

The dangerous jungle of Lawn

Taking a last look at Stumps to place him, he crept out of his room, down the stairs, and through the kitchen. He unbolted the back door and stepped out into the moonlight. His sharp eyes searched the yard. There he was. It was certainly Stumps, standing still, his shadow like a little clothespin. Max wondered whether it felt terrifying to be so little in such a huge world under such an enormous moon-washed sky! He thought of all the other small creatures, mice, toads, beetles, some much tinier than Stumps, ants and spiders and furry caterpillars. To God, no doubt Max seemed just as small and in need of help. Max felt he would like to protect all little creatures, and wondered who did. His job now was to protect Stumps.

Max felt so pleased that Stumps was found that he was about to hurry over and swoop on him and carry him up to his safe attic. It seemed so easy to do this, and surely the poor Duke of York (as he used to be) had suffered enough hardships.

But then Max had a great longing to see if Stumps would manage for himself, would notice the creeper and be able to climb that twisty thick trunk up to his window! There Max could take him in and rescue him.

Even as Max was thinking all this, Stumps began to hurry toward the vine. Max watched him until he couldn't tell Stumps from the pointed leaves into which the soldier had dived. Then Max hurried back to his room and leaned out of the window.

Far below him he could hear a rustle, a scrape and a shiver in the creeper. The sounds came slowly closer and closer, a shuffle and a ruffle of leaves. Max thought he could make out a thin, breathless tune.

"Boney was a warrior . . ." then a long pause. Then a little grunt as Stumps found a foothold. "Boney was a warrior. . . ." Then very slowly as the singer wriggled himself up the trunk, "way . . . yay . . . yah." Then more briskly as he swung from twig to close twig on his feet:

> "Boney was a warrior
> John France wah!
> Boney beat . . . the Rooshians
> Way—ay-yah
> Boney beat the Rooshians,
> John France—wah!"

Then a long, scrambling pause, and the singer started again:

> "Boney went to Mossycow . . .
> Way—ay-yah
> Boney he came back again.
> John France—wah! Whoops!"

A tiny slither and a breathless gasp. Then the thin voice rose, braver than before and nearer.

> "Boney went to Waterloo
> Way—ay—YAH
> Boney went to Waterloo,
> John France—wah!"

But when Boney broke his heart and died, Max heard Stump's voice below him, as plaintive as a humming gnat.

Nearer Stumps climbed, until at last Max saw the leaves twitch close at hand and he stepped out into the moonlight on the piece of straight trunk trained past Max's window.

Max knew he must be discreet and gentle now, or he would frighten him and make him topple off into the yard.

"Well done, Stumps, once King of the Twelves," he whispered; and he put his hand out very quietly and grasped him. "The Genie has you in his hand."

Stumps must have understood, for he neither struggled nor went wooden. Max looked at Stumps closely for the first time. His main oddities were his round turnipy head and his stumpy, rather bandy, legs. Max smiled; he loved Stumps. He carried him up the attic stairs, opened the door, and put him down on the highway of moonlight which led to his companions.

7

The Four Kings of Ashanti

MAX woke with a sense of excitement and in a flash remembered all about the return of Stumps. He swung out of bed.

"Stumps, Stumps, good old Stumps," he chanted, like the soldiers, flinging on his clothes. Frederic Guelph—I think that's what they said. What a queer name—Frederic Guelph, Duke of York, Frederic the First, Frederic the Second. I wonder if all the time, underneath, he wished he could go on being king when he gave his crown to that old Duke of Wellington?

Max sat on the bed, tying his shoes, and he suddenly thought, I wonder who made all this up? Because they know all sorts of things about themselves. They know their names and their ages and all about going to Africa. Could they make it all up themselves? Butter could perhaps. But no, I don't think so. I think it's the Genii who have to make things up. The way I do. The way I did about Stumps wandering around the kitchen and getting out of Brutus' door. And then it was really true. He really had.

It didn't seem odd to Max that what he had imagined about Stumps was really true, because this was exactly how the games you made up worked. Of course they were true. In your mind. It was only that this had gone one step more and come alive, and he could watch it.

"All that about Ashanti and Africa," he muttered. "That would need a Genie. And I didn't make that up. There must have been another Genie, and I bet it was some boy who had them before. Before someone hid them under the floorboard."

Max wondered who this boy was so long ago. Over a hundred years ago, his father had said. Then he remembered that before they came downstairs, Butter Crashey had said that they had gone to Africa under the protection of the four Genii. Four. Then were there *four* boys? Or there might have been some girls. After all, he wouldn't mind Jane playing; she would make a good Genie. She loved making things up. Perhaps these boys of a hundred years ago had a sister. The next time he had the chance, Max determined to ask the patriarch about the four Genii who used to protect them.

They would all know that he had searched for and protected Stumps and guided him back. He was longing to go and see them, but there wasn't time before breakfast. Max had overslept after his wakeful night.

He ran down to the dining room and flumped into his place. He wasn't quite last; he and Philip had a battle on the stairs, and Max won.

"What a noise, boys," Mrs. Morley said.

"Noise-boys-boise-noys-noise-boise," yelled Max. He felt fine.

"You seem full of the devil," said his father. "What is it?"

"Stumps is found, by the way," Max said.

"Who's Stumps?" Jane asked.

"My wooden soldier."

"Oh good, Maxy. I am relieved," his mother said. "Mr. Howson thinks they may really be valuable. So let that teach you to look after them."

"My whole life," said Max solemnly, "is to be given up to protecting them."

"I hope your whole life won't be spent in the attic, darling. It's such lovely weather. You've been stuck up there ever since you found them."

"Well, I like playing with them."

"Bring them down into the garden."

Max considered this in silence.

"What did you call him? Stumps?" asked Philip, having satisfied his hunger a little with three large spoonfuls of cornflakes.

"Yes."

"Why?"

"Why not? Because he's got stumpy legs, I guess."

"And all on his stumps he begs," roared Philip, down the scale.

"Not at the table," said Mr. Morley.

"He's got lots of other names anyway."

"Have they all got names?" Jane asked.

"Yes, but I don't know them all."

71

"You mean you haven't thought of enough," she said.

This wasn't what Max meant, but he didn't say so.

"One's Butter, isn't it?" Philip said.

"How do you know?" asked Max.

"I heard you tell Mr. Howson. I distinctly heard you say 'Butter's a hundred and forty.' I blushed for your childish imaginings," Philip said, "but Mr. Rochester didn't notice."

Mr. Howson had become Mr. Rochester to them all. Jane was looking forward to going to church in order to stare at him again.

By the time Max was free to go up to the attic after doing his chores, it was nearly the middle of the morning. Philip had gone off over the purpling moors on his bicycle. Jane had disappeared somewhere. His mother was safely in the kitchen, cooking and talking to Mrs. Hodgson. His father was in the farmyard. Max hoped very much that his mother wouldn't return to her idea of his bringing Butter and Company down, because he couldn't safely do this yet. Anybody might see them, and then the secret would be out—the excitement of having it for himself over. Or what would be worse, they might laugh and disbelieve, and then the precious wooden soldiers might freeze forever.

Max thought this was quite possible. And he didn't yet know when they would freeze or when they wouldn't. They might run, as they had done from the kitchen table. It was dangerous. He must play with them up there, even though it was hot and sunny and he would have liked to go with Phil to explore their

72

new neighborhood. He had brought a little pale blue flag on a pin from a flag-day collection. It seemed right for the soldiers.

He approached the attic quietly and saw, to his surprise, that the door was slightly open. Could he have left it unlatched last night when he put Stumps back? If so, it was careless of him, and dangerous. Supposing they had all trooped down to the hall and been stepped on?

Max pushed the door open quietly. He was delighted to see that the soldiers were already on the move. Something important seemed to be afoot. So they didn't always need the drum to rouse them. Perhaps, Max thought, the more he did with them the more active they would be. After all, they had been out of practice for over a hundred years, he supposed.

He crept in, closed the door, and then saw that he couldn't take his usual place on the Ashanti stool, because they were gathered around it. Max put the flag down near the stool, squatted quietly on the floor, and watched. The patriarch seemed to be directing operations. He was leading a small band of men over to the pile of balsa wood which Philip used to make things. Max looked at the soldiers.

Those are Monkey, Crackey and Tracky, the midshipmen, he said to himself. These three, with Butter to help, ranged themselves on each side of a long thin strip of balsa, picked it up as Butter said "Heave!" and began to carry it toward the Ashanti stool.

They tramped past Max, panting heavily. They heaved the plank up so that it made a ramp onto the

Ashanti stool, and at this point Bravey, Gravey and Cheeky were there to help.

They're trying to climb onto it, Max thought. And then he remembered about the kings of Ashanti being crowned on it. He wondered if this was why they wanted to climb on. He could see Stumps sitting on the floor and leaning nonchalantly against the wall of the Ashanti canoe, with his short legs crossed.

In another group, evidently waiting for action, was the Duke of Wellington himself, or rather the King, as Max now knew. With the Duke was the lively, jaunty soldier who had first wakened the others to life, and whose name Max badly wanted to find out. The two other nameless soldiers were also there, chatting to the Duke and looking haughty and important. As Max watched, the jaunty fellow flung out his arms, pointed his toe, and put his head on one side, as if he were acting a part.

Perhaps I'll find out who they are this time, Max thought.

The ramp was now in position, held by six men. At the patriarch's word, three left it and hurried over to Max's old bricks with which he sometimes made forts. They got behind one and pushed it across the floor to hold firm the end of the ramp.

"Good idea," Max said. "Now what happens?"

What happened was that the Duke of Wellington scrambled onto the ramp and began the perilous ascent to the Ashanti stool.

"Goodness, he'll never do it," Max muttered.

The balsa wood was smooth and slippery. The poor Duke slipped and scrambled up his improvised gang-

74

way, often going down on his knees and barely saving himself.

"This won't do for a king," Max said. He began to sing, very softly, the Duke of York's song.

> "And when he was up, he was up
> And when he was down he was down
> And when he was only halfway up
> He was neither up nor down."

Max sang, strictly in time, to a brisk rhythm. The Duke seemed to take heart, stood up, held out his arms, marched boldly ahead—bouncing gently with the ramp—and at last stepped onto the curved seat of the stool in triumph.

"Hooray," said Max, very gently.

"Hooray!" echoed the Twelves from below. One by one, the three other nameless soldiers stepped onto the gangway. Max piped them aboard the stool with his song until all four stood aloft, facing the others on the floor. The patriarch went last, and though one hundred and forty, he showed the same uprightness and agility that he had shown going downstairs. He settled himself cross-legged, in a patriarchal way, in front of the four others.

Butter held up his hands for silence.

"Now that the four kings—Sneaky, Wellington, Parry and Ross—are enthroned," he said, "you may begin the review and the triumphal entry of Stumps."

Sneaky isn't a very kinglike name, Max couldn't help thinking. I wonder if the lively fellow is Sneaky? It's just the kind of name I'd give a soldier, and perhaps he became a king later.

Monkey scuttled over to beat the Ashanti drum, which lay beside the stool, and saw the flag. He let out a shrill yelp of glee, pounced on it, and waved it.

There was a slight argument as to who should bear the colors, and Max saw Bravey grasp the flag by sheer elbowing power. Cheeky and Gravey fell in to support him, and the color party set forth, the two midshipmen behind. They marched past the stool to the tiny sound of Monkey's tattoo, *tum tiddle um tum, tum tiddle um tum,* saluting as they passed the kings, who were solemnly saluting back. The patriarch didn't salute, but held up both hands, with palms facing, in a kind of blessing, to show that he was different.

Then the column went on, picked up Stumps, and proceeding to the other side of the attic, swung around and began a straightforward march to the stool again.

It was then that Max saw Jane. (He had watched them around, of course, turning his head.) Her white face was peering at him from behind some furniture. Her blue eyes were round as medals. She was pale to the lips, and her mouth was open.

"Max!" she hissed softly.

Max was horrified, much more because he thought Jane's presence would stop this wonderful parade than because he felt angry. He hadn't time to feel angry.

"Be quiet," he whispered in a tone of fierce command. "Keep still." Then he turned his attention to the Twelves. They had reached the ramp, halted, and presented Stumps. Stumps bowed; the soldiers cheered. Monkey beat a wild last tattoo, the four kings inclined their heads in a martial way, and the patriarch nodded three times. The Twelves chanted:

> "Frederic Guelph Duke of York
> Frederic the First, King of the Twelves
> Afterwards made Frederic the Second
> Stumps, Stumps, here is Stumps
> Stumps, Stumps, back from the grave."

"Hail, Stumpy. Hail, Knockhead."

"Never mind your bandy legs!" piped Bravey saucily. Other soldiers quickly muffled him, and the patriarch pretended not to notice. Stumps merely smiled in a lofty way, secure in his kingship.

Well, thought Max, I'm glad they give him some honor, even if he did give up being king.

"Tell your tale, Stumps," said Butter.

Everyone stood at ease, including Monkey. Stumps stepped forward and told his tale. Max had to lean down and listen hard to hear the words, for he hadn't heard Stumps speak before.

Stumps' adventures were what Max had imagined, in every way. Stumps didn't know what the S bend below the sink was called, and he referred to it as a great white creeper in the crook of which he was safe. (This must be because he's so used to Africa, thought Max, where they have great twisty creepers.) He was even safe from a roaring animal that pursued things over the floor, sucking up everything into its path. (Mrs. Hodgson's vacuum cleaner.) When he had finished with the account of his climb to safety,

Well donel

BERNARDA
BRYSON

everyone clapped and cheered and broke ranks. It seemed the assembly was over.

"Maxy," said Jane. "I don't understand."

"Follow me out," he whispered, "and don't walk near them."

He tiptoed to the door. Jane followed. Max shut the Twelves in to finish their rejoicings, and faced her on the landing.

8

Alexander Sneaky

MAX looked at Jane with a kind of triumph. It was sad, in a way, that his secret was over. Now that he had time to think of it, it was mean of Jane to have hidden like that. Nevertheless, there was no question of Jane's not believing or laughing at him. She had seen it with her own eyes.

Jane was frightened and bewildered. She was looking at Max as if he were a person she hadn't known before.

"How do you do it?" she said huskily.

"At first," Max said, "it was when I beat the Ashanti drum. But this time they did it on their own. They came downstairs too. That time I was in the kitchen and you all came back and Stumps got lost. He hid, you see. Jane, you've really got to promise not to tell anyone else. Yet. After all, it was pretty sneaky to hide like that."

"I know," Jane said. "I didn't mean to. I was just going to get the rest of my books from that trunk, and then I heard you coming and I thought it would be fun to hear your game. Because you wouldn't tell me. But I didn't know it was *this* kind of a secret," she added.

The color had come back into her cheeks. Max took these tiny, lively creatures for granted. He didn't seem frightened by their doings, so she needn't be. The strangeness of the little soldiers began to be overcome in her mind by the same excitement and delight that Max felt.

"Max, I'm sorry I hid," she went on. "But it's *marvelous!*"

Max nodded. He was satisfied because Jane was so impressed.

"You can be a Genie, too, if you like," he said generously, "and watch over them."

"What's a Genie? Like *The Arabian Nights?*"

"Sort of. I'm one. I look after them and they consult me. At least Butter does."

"Is Butter the most important?"

"His real name's Butter Crashey. He's the patriarch, one hundred and forty. And he's the oracle for them. He comes to ask me things."

"How did you think of Butter Crashey?"

"I didn't *think* of it. He told me," Max said, with scorn. "They know their names. And their ages. And they remember all about an expedition to Africa and a kingdom they had there. They tell me. What I think," he went on as he and Jane sat on the top stair, "is this. That the boys who had them before and who were their Genii made all this up."

"I see. What boys?"

"Well, some family must have had them. Over a hundred years ago, as Daddy said. And Butter says there were four. Four Genii. Or it may have been some girls too," he said kindly, "so I guess you could be a Genie. If you wanted."

"I do," Jane said. "They're *sweet*."

"You mustn't call them sweet," Max replied. "Soldiers wouldn't like it. And they don't like my helping them too much, either. They have to do things their own way. Look, Jane, promise you won't tell anyone. Yet."

Jane put her hand on Max's.

"I absolutely swear," she said.

"I'm going back to ask B. Crashey about those other three kings. I didn't know till today that there were four kings."

"May I come?" Jane pleaded.

"Not this time. I'll ask him about your being a Genie, okay? You see, they're not used to you yet."

"All right," Jane said. "I'll wait here."

Max was gone for a long time, and then the telephone rang and their mother called her. Casting a longing glance at the closed attic door, Jane went down.

Max had gone back into the attic, sat on the stool, which was now deserted, and picked up Butter Crashey. The rest had moved the ramp from the stool to the Ashanti canoe, and with whoops of delight, were climbing aboard it.

"I enjoyed the parade," Max began.

Butter Crashey seemed pleased, and his wise, wrinkled patriarchal face creased into an endearing

82

smile. It was the first time Max had noticed his smile.

"We knew that you would be present, Oh Protector of Stumps," he said.

"Butter Crashey, tell me about the other three kings. I know about Arthur Wellesley, Duke of Wellington, scourge of Napoleon," Max said, thinking this sounded very grand. "But why were there four kings?"

"We divided our kingdom among the Ashanti into four parts," the patriarch explained. "Therefore, there were four kings."

"Oh, I see," Max said. And added eagerly, "Were there four kings because there were four Genii?" He had just thought of this.

Butter Crashey nodded wisely.

"No doubt," he said, "that was why. One to protect each king and each country."

"Of course," Max agreed. "I suppose the Genii chose the kings?"

"It is lost in the ancient days of the Young Men. But our legends say that the four Genii seized upon four chosen warriors, promised to protect them, and told them that they would one day all be kings."

I'd choose Stumps, Max thought.

"Do the legends say what the names of the Genii were?" he asked. If he knows this, thought Max, I shall find out about the boy or boys who had them so long ago.

Butter looked shocked.

"We have all known the names of the Genii," he protested, "since time out of mind."

"Can you tell me what they were?" Max asked boldly.

"The chief Genie's was Brannii. The others were Tallii, Emmii and Annii."

Max sighed. They were very made-up names, but of course he would have expected that.

"Did they live here in this very place?" he asked.

"Who can say where the Genii live? They are not confined to houses but often reside in the desert or the hills or the strange places of the clouds," Butter said soberly. "All the same," he added in a more practical tone, "their abode wasn't very far from here."

"And do you know, Butter Crashey," Max asked next, "which Genie chose which soldier?"

"Who should know but I?" said the patriarch. "It was after the building of our first town in Africa. I had gone into the desert to seek out the Genii. While the rest were sitting together in the common hall, the air suddenly darkened, the hall shook, and continual streams of fire flashed through the room, followed by long and loud peals of thunder. You may read it in *The History of the Young Men*," he said. Max was disappointed, for he was afraid that the patriarch had finished speaking and he didn't know where to find *The History of the Young Men*, even if there really was such a book.

"What happened next?" he asked eagerly.

"A dreadful monster entered the room with me in his hand. He put me down gently (for although the Genii are terrible to us in power, we have learned to

84

know that they are kindly disposed) and said, in a loud voice . . ." Butter paused.

"Yes?" Max whispered.

"I am the chief Genie Brannii. With me there are three others; she who protects you, Wellesley, is named Tallii; she who protects Parry is named Emmii; she who protects Ross is called Annii. We are the guardians of this land; we are the guardians of you all. Revere this man Crashey. He is entrusted with secrets you can never know." At this point Crashey winked very solemnly, yet Max thought he could detect a twinkle in his black mouselike eyes. "Then he spread out his dragon wings and flew away," said the patriarch.

"So," said Max, who had been listening intently, "there was one boy Genie and three girl Genii?"

"That is so," Butter said.

One boy, Max thought, and three sisters.

"And now in these degenerate days," the patriarch added rather sadly, "we are reduced to one Genie only. Yourself, Oh Maxii. How are the mighty fallen," he added, sniffing.

Max liked Maxii; it sounded much more like a Genie.

"A new Genie has come," he explained, "whose name is Janeii."

Butter looked very pleased and nodded.

"Come, that's better," he said, dropping his oracle manner. "We shall be more protected, and such accidents as befell Stumps lately may be prevented."

"Butter Crashey," Max asked, "which soldier did the chief Genie protect? Was it Sneaky, the very lively one? Do you know, right at the beginning I saw him make you alive. I mean—" Max stopped, confused. "It looked as if he woke you all up."

"No wonder," Butter said, not at all offended. "Alexander Sneaky it is, and he was the favorite of Chief Genie Brannii, the redheaded. He is certainly lively, though he has moods and strikes attitudes. He is ingenious, artful, deceitful but courageous," explained the patriarch. "No wonder he woke us up. Did we not live under the protection of Chief Genie Brannii? And Sneaky is his man."

"Of course. I see," Max answered. And he thought to himself that the chief Genie must have started the game and kept it going, and perhaps the soldiers were really his, since he was the boy.

"And Parry?" Max said. "What's he like?"

"There he is, climbing the prow of that ship now, by a secret way," said Butter, pointing. Parry had scorned the ramp, and scrambling over some books and papers, was about to drop down over the bow and take the others by surprise.

"He is fifteen and a brave sailorlike young man, but a little too fond of subterfuge," Butter said.

What sneaks these kings seem to be, thought Max, but it's better than all being the same dull old heroes.

"How are the mighty fallen!" said Butter again as Tracky shot up from the canoe and knocked Parry smartly down to the ground again with a piece of balsa. Max laughed, and even the patriarch was seen to smile.

"And Ross, what's Ross doing?" Max asked.

"There he is, standing on the gunwale. Sixteen

years, frank, open, honest and of a bravery in battle sometimes approaching to madness. Though I admit he is a queer little thing to look at, he was the protected of the Genie Annii."

One sister, thought Max, was called Anne.

"Maxy, Maxy!" called his mother, and it sounded as if her feet were on the very stairs to the attic.

"Help!" Max gasped. He put the patriarch down in the boat, and dashed from the room with a clatter and a bang.

And that, he thought as he ran to the stairs, is what they call thunder.

9

Mr. Rochester

THE telephone call had been from Mrs. Rochester (as Jane now called her), asking them to tea. Their mother never accepted invitations for the children without making sure that they hadn't arranged anything else, and even more important, that they wanted to go. She had asked Jane, and now she asked Max.

He met her on the first landing, and they went downstairs together.

"Do *you* want to go, Janey?" Max asked. He was hoping she would say she didn't, because he had looked forward to their first time together with the Young Men. On the other hand, he had liked Mr. Howson.

Jane knew what Max was thinking, but just the same she wanted to go.

"Yes, I do," she said.

"Why? Just because you think he's like that old Mr. Rochester?" Max said rather grumpily.

Jane grinned. "Well, you liked him," she said. "You told me so."

"He was interested in my soldiers," Max explained.

"Yes, he's a great antiquarian," said Mrs. Morley, "and sometime you must show them to him."

"What's a great antiquarium?" Max asked, in tones of disgust. He often sounded disgusted when he didn't understand something.

"A person who loves and knows about old things," she explained.

"*I* thought it had to do with fishes," Max said unbelievingly.

"That's an aquarium," said his mother.

Max looked at Jane sideways.

"First he's an old brontyfan with a great long neck," he said, "and then he's an antiquarium with fishes swimming around inside him." He was trying to make Jane laugh and succeeding. She was excited anyway, and now she began to giggle until Max joined in, and they both laughed until Mrs. Morley had to laugh too. Max and Jane, with red faces, were pushing each other around in the hall when Philip walked in.

"What's the joke?" he said. "You silly little things!"

"Phil," Jane gasped, "do you want to go to tea with Mr. and Mrs. Rochester?"

"No," said Philip at once. "Thanks," he added.

"Oh, Philip," his mother said, "I've got to call them back. What can I say? Besides, I don't imagine you'll see much of them; they're really asking you so you can get to know their children. There's a boy a little younger than you are and—you'll never guess. There are triplets—girls!"

The three Morleys seemed stunned by this information. They stared at their mother.

"*That's* not a bit like Mr. Rochester," Jane said solemnly and in an outraged tone.

"Why didn't you *tell* us?" said Max, who thought that triplets were so unusual as to be worth going to see.

"I haven't had a chance yet, with you two being so silly."

"Anyway," Philip put in gloomily, "what difference do triplets make? How old?"

"About Jane's age."

"It'll be Jane multiplied by three," Philip said, making a face at her. "One's enough."

"Let's go," said Jane.

"Shall we, Maxy? We'll be outnumbered by one," Philip said.

"All right," said Max, pleased to find himself bracketed with Philip. "Where have you been?"

Mrs. Morley went to the telephone with a feeling of relief.

"All over the place," Phil said. "The heather's gorgeous, and I've been through Haworth, where all these old Brontë fans go, and seen the parsonage where the Brontës lived."

"Did you go in?" Jane asked.

"No, I'll wait till Mummy takes us. Then she'll pay," he said softly, winking at his sister.

Philip was inclined to be careful with his money.

Mrs. Morley was right. They didn't see much of

90

the Reverend and Mrs. Howson at first, for they were greeted in the parsonage drive by the young Howsons and at once taken on a tour of both the house and garden, a procedure that seems necessary before two English families get to know each other. Christopher Howson was tall and pale like his father, and he and Philip rushed off, talking hard.

"Come on," Philip yelled.

The triplets, who were alike and not alike, surrounded Jane and began to ask if she were coming to their school as all the girls followed their brothers.

Max trailed along behind, rather forlorn, beginning to wish he hadn't come. He would rather have been with the Twelves. There was Jane, the new Genie, and she had completely forgotten them.

"Max! Keep up with us," Philip called. "We need you against this monstrous regiment of women."

Max didn't quite understand this, but he knew that for the moment it meant boys against girls, and anyway it made a big difference to his feelings. He tore past the girls, making a noise like a train whistle, and caught up to Philip and Christopher.

The visitors were shown the best trees to climb and the views from the top. They inspected a small greenhouse, a cave, and a private loose brick in a wall where the girls posted secret letters. Christopher's tour included the orchard, where Max stole an apple, and the cabbages and the lawn and the chickens.

Then they raced for the house and entered it like a tornado. By this time everybody knew everybody, nobody was shy, and their seven voices—all talking at once and shouting to be heard—filled the parsonage with a roaring noise. Each door they came to was rushed at by a Howson and the room introduced as if it were a person. More often than not, Christopher and one or another of his sisters had a fight at the doorknob. Doors slammed or swung behind them as they impatiently went on to the next.

Jane had a feeling that this wasn't a very polite way to go out to tea, but there was no doubt that it left no room for shyness. She was behind the others, who had just charged upstairs. Max was far too excited, stamping. There was a door next to the living room which nobody had opened. Perhaps it wouldn't hurt to peep inside. She turned the handle gently and looked in.

Over by the window stood the tall, black, somber figure of the parson, gazing out at the jagged cedar tree and lost, it was certain, in his own thoughts.

"Oh, Mr. Rochester, I'm sorry," Jane gasped.

He had turned around and was looking at her without seeing her, it seemed, his eyes dark in his pale face. At least, that was what Jane thought.

"Come in, come in, Jane," he said, and he laughed. "*What* did you call me?" Jane walked into the room very gently and gracefully, as she always did, not knowing quite what to say. She looked at her feet and then up at Mr. Howson.

"Mr. Rochester," she said softly. "We call you Mr. Rochester at home because I think you're like him, and I'm sorry, I got mixed up."

"And do you know who I think you're like?" he said. "I think you're like Jane Eyre."

Jane looked pleased and smiled.

"Have you just been reading it?" he asked.

"Yes. I love it. I love Mr. Rochester. I'm going to begin reading it again."

"Most girls like Mr. Rochester," he said. "I suppose because he's so mysterious."

Jane nodded. She didn't know why she liked him, but this might be one reason. Her face was flushed from racing around the garden, and glowing with her ideas about Mr. Rochester. Mr. Howson thought to himself that Jane would soon grow up into a beautiful girl and have to marry a quite ordinary man like himself, like any man, and not at all like the amazing Mr. Rochester. He prayed to God there and then to send her a good, true one who would value the flame inside her and not dim it. He laughed again as a clatter of feet sounded overhead.

"Aren't we making a noise?" Jane said. "Will Mrs. Howson mind? They're showing us the house."

"No, she won't mind. See you at tea, Jane," he said, waving, and she whirled around, light as a feather, and skipped out.

At tea, Max was very talkative. It must have been racing round the garden, clattering through the attics, and sliding down the bannisters. Or perhaps it was the game of miniature golf they had played afterward. Whatever it was, he felt thoroughly at home and very friendly toward Mr. Howson who was sitting next to him.

"I found the lost soldier," he said.

"Oh, did you, Max? I'm glad of that. Now tell me again, where did you find these soldiers?"

Max told the tale and he told it well, describing

how he had stepped on the squeaky, uneven board. By the time he had finished, everybody was listening.

"And inside this old roll of rag were all the soldiers," he said, "one by one."

"And Max has done nothing but stick in the attic playing with them ever since," said Philip, "and Mummy thinks it's unhealthy."

"I can remember being crazy about soldiers," Christopher said, as if this were years and years ago.

"And what do you do with them?" asked Mrs. Howson.

"Oh, Mummy! You set them all out and parade them and kill them off in battles and make them alive again and bomb them and take them on forced marches and all that."

"And you give them all names," Philip said. "Field Marshall So and So and Major General What's-It."

Max was staring at Jane with bright, mischievous gray eyes. And Jane was smiling back with wide, secretive blue ones. She had forgotten all about Mr. Rochester and remembered the wonderful secret. Max laughed out of sheer pleasure because these people didn't know. They didn't know that he didn't have to do things, that Butter and the Duke and the others, especially Stumps, did things on their own.

"But Maxy's names are the nuttiest you ever heard," Philip went on. "Butter, for instance."

"Butter!" shrieked one of the triplets. "Why?"

"For one reason," Max said quickly, "he fell in the butter."

"Max," Mr. Howson said, "remind me to tell you about the Brontë family, who lived at Haworth near

"I fell into the butter long ago."

here. When they were small, they had soldiers. And they had such vivid imaginations that they made up the most exciting adventures for their soldiers to have."

"Did they?" Max asked. "How do you know?"

"We know because they were born writers and wrote it down. Even when they were quite young. And it went on for years and years. There are books and books of it; notebooks, you know, some so tiny you can hardly see the writing. I think Branwell and Charlotte wrote the most, but they all played these games. Jane knows about Charlotte. She's been reading *Jane Eyre*, she tells me. I can't remember the names of all the stories, but I know one was called *The History of the Young Men*."

Max had stopped chewing and was gazing at Mr. Howson in astonishment, his mouth open.

"Max, swallow your cake," Philip said, nudging him.

"And they gave all theirs names, too, of course. Some were after famous people, and some were just fun, like yours. In fact, I'm not sure one of theirs wasn't Butter. Butter Something. I guess that's what reminded me. I must look it up again."

Max closed his mouth and gazed at his plate and took another piece of bread and butter and said absolutely nothing. He didn't dare look at Jane. He felt himself turning red. Then he felt himself feeling faint and fluttery, the way he did when he knew he had done something wrong and was about to be found out and blamed. Mr. Howson thought that he had bored Max by talking of things he didn't know about, and Mrs. Howson thought that there was a sudden silence and she had better fill it. And Philip thought Max was behaving very oddly, not to say rudely. And the Howson family thought their father should be stopped when he began to talk about the Brontës. So they all suddenly started to say things together, and then everyone laughed and tried again, and the awkward moment passed. Max's wooden soldiers were forgotten—by everyone but Max and Jane.

10

The Four Genii

"JANEY, come up to the attic," Max whispered as they put their bicycles away. Philip had already gone off toward the farmyard.

Jane nodded eagerly, and Max felt relieved. She hadn't forgotten; she was still a faithful Genie.

Without talking, they pelted up the stairs, and as Mrs. Morley came out of the kitchen to ask them if they had enjoyed themselves she thought, Ah, Jane's in Max's game now, evidently. And she wondered what it was that absorbed them so.

"Wasn't it funny about the Brontës having soldiers?" Jane said softly as they approached the attic door.

"*Funny,*" said Max in a tone heavy with excitement and meaning. "Janey, do you realize that thing he said they wrote, called *The History of the Young Men*, is what Butter talked about this morning?"

Jane stared at Max.

"You didn't tell me."

door. But now their impatience had made their voices grow louder and louder. Max suddenly realized this.

"Shush!" he said.

"Well, you shush," retorted Jane, with reason. "Wait here, don't go in without me, and I'll go and ask Mummy."

Max promised to wait. But he couldn't resist kneeling down and looking through the keyhole.

There wasn't a soldier to be seen. The space before the Ashanti stool was empty. He couldn't see the whole attic from the keyhole, and he had promised not to go in.

Jane returned to find him kneeling before the door. She was breathless and as she knelt, too, she giggled.

"This is how I saw you when you first started it, and you had that candy ball."

"I *didn't* start it," Max protested. "They've gone," he added. "What are the names?"

"What do you mean, *gone*?" Jane said, shocked, pushing him aside and putting an eye to the keyhole. "Max!"

"Well, they walk around. We'll go in soon. What are the four names?"

Jane raised her head.

"Charlotte, Branwell, Emily and Anne," she said. "In that order. There were two older ones that died."

Max looked at her, remembering.

"Well, the Genii were called Brannii, Tallii, Emmii and Annii," he said slowly.

They both squatted back on their heels.

"The only one that isn't right is Tallii," Jane said.

"Brannii was the chief Genie. That's the boy. Branwell, isn't it?"

"Yes. He was Patrick Branwell, but as their father was Patrick, too, he was called Branwell, Mummy said."

"Was she suspicious?"

"No, she just said she supposed Mr. Rochester had got us interested, and I said yes. I was as vague as anything."

"Good. I'd already guessed Anne. Emmii is Emily. So, Tallii must be the Charlotte one."

"It ought to be Charlii."

"Well, I guess she thought that was too much like a boy."

"Yes."

"You see, Butter called me Maxii, and then I called you Janeii."

"All to go with Genii," Jane added.

"Let's go in and I'll say you're here!"

"Yes," Jane said, very excited. "Max, may I hold one, the way you do?"

"I think you might hold Butter. He's the one who's used to speaking to the Genii. We'll see what happens."

They went in and looked all around the attic in each corner. No Young Men.

"Maybe they're behind something," Max whispered.

"Where do you keep them? In that shoe box?"

"Yes, but they wouldn't put themselves away."

"They could. Oh, Max." She clutched his arm. "They're in the boat!"

They were. Only the heads and shoulders of the Twelves showed above the sides of the carved canoe. Their heads were bent on their hands, and their hands were clutching balsa-wood oars which rested on their little knees and over the sides of the canoe. They were asleep, it seemed.

"Worn out with rowing," Max whispered. Butter sat in the bow, his head bent forward on his chest. Crackey sat in the stern, or rather leaned back, sleeping comfortably. Between them sat the others, in two rows of five, holding their oars of different lengths and looking like galley slaves.

Max and Jane kneeled down to look at them.

"Have they gone back to being wooden?" Jane asked.

Max looked at Butter fixedly. As he looked he could make out, perhaps, the slightest rise and fall of his breathing. He wasn't sure.

Then he looked at Crackey's face—the only face that showed—and realized that he had known it was Crackey, which meant his face wasn't wooden and blurred but lively and detailed. "No. They're just asleep," he said.

At this moment the patriarch woke, stretched his arms, yawned, rubbed his eyes and said in a brisk voice, "Ready all."

"Oh, his darling yawn," said Jane.

"Jane, don't treat him like a toy or a baby animal, please," Max warned. He felt that this would be wrong and insulting. "He's a small, alive person," he explained, "and full of years and wisdom. He says so."

"Yes, I see," Jane said meekly.

At his words, all the others sat up, balanced their oars as best they could without rowlocks—many finding them too heavy—and began to row rather wildly as Butter directed.

"One, two; one, two; one, two," said the patriarch briskly.

"Mind your elbows, Cheeky," growled Gravey.

"Old sourpuss," retorted the bold Cheeky.

"I should be obliged if His present Majesty could keep his knees out of my back," Stumps requested of the Duke of Wellington.

"Impossible to achieve," drawled the Duke, "since you push your back into my knees."

"Brave Benbow lost his legs by chain shot, by chain sho-o-ot," yelled Crackey from the stern, to the time of the rowing.

"Move over, Ross," Parry snarled.

"How can I? The boat's curved and throws you into the middle like a feather bed," said Ross angrily. With all this argument, the rowing became wilder and wilder. Max and Jane watched, half-smiling and half-alarmed as the cries and arguments of the twelve grew louder. Sneaky found it impossible to row properly sitting down, so he leaped up and began using his piece of wood like a punt pole over the side, to the peril of Tracky, who sat in his way.

"That's Sneaky," Max whispered, "and he was the favorite of Chief Genie Brannii. Butter told me so. He's one of the kings, do you remember?"

"He would be," said Jane.

102

"We're not getting far anyway," Monkey said, "without any water."

"You look as if you're waving a flag, not rowing a boat," said Cheeky.

Monkey raised his oar, which was certainly short, and brought it down crack on Cheeky's head. Cheeky returned the blow, but his oar glanced off and hit Gravey. Gravey howled, stood up, and began hitting everyone at random, still with an expression of utmost melancholy. Sneaky was quick to join him.

At once there was pandemonium in the Ashanti canoe as all the rowers jumped up.

"Help," said Jane, "how do you stop a quarrel?"

"I've never had to. Butter usually does," Max whispered.

Butter was standing up with raised arms, calling "Easy all," but nobody took much notice. They went on whacking and punching with great abandon, and the canoe was rocking a little on the attic floor.

Max swooped on Butter and lifted him high.

"Command silence, Oh Patriarch," he suggested.

The patriarch blinked, but finding himself in a position of such advantage, he said loudly, "Pray silence!" As they heard this voice, apparently from the courts of heaven, the Twelves stopped fighting, sat down, and rubbed their bruises.

"Butter Crashey," said Max solemnly, "the Genie Janeii is present." He could hardly keep from laughing, Genie Janeii sounded so funny.

The patriarch's wise wrinkled face took on a look of satisfaction. Jane was watching intently, smiling.

Max held Butter toward her, signaling to her to take him.

Jane put her finger and thumb around his body, and felt the taut, thrilling wriggle of life. She couldn't help a slight shiver.

"Welcome, Oh Genii, on behalf of the Young Men," the patriarch said. He bowed his top half in her hand and looked up smilingly. Jane smiled back. His eyes were as bright and beady as those of a mouse. She was enchanted.

"I am glad to be here, Oh Patriarch," she replied with natural grace, having noted the way Max addressed him.

From the boat came the sound of a thin cheer. All malice and sulks seemed to be over.

"They welcome you," said Butter Crashey, nodding.

"Put him back in the boat, Jane," Max whispered as they heard their mother ring the bell for supper. Jane did so, and as they crept from the attic they heard the Young Men's voices rise in a sea song.

"We'll rant and we'll roar," they shrilled, "all o'er the wild ocean . . ."

"Max, the *feel* of him," Jane said as they ran downstairs.

"I know. You can always tell when they freeze. They feel wooden again."

"Yes, I see. I love the way they sing."

"Now listen to this," said Mr. Morley when the plates were filled. He reached behind him and brought out a newspaper. "Just listen. Here we are, 'Letters to the Editor.' " He began to read:

"Sir,

Is it too much to hope that somewhere, lurking unrecognized in some attic or farmhouse or parsonage, or perhaps treasured but unknown among the objects in a living-room cabinet, there may survive some of the original wooden soldiers, Napoleonic in outfit and design, which— I would rather say who—inspired the children of Haworth with their earliest, fertile imaginings?

Where are the noble Twelves, the Young Men, beloved of Branwell and his sisters, who, with their imaginary descendants, peopled all the early stories of this brilliant family? Could we but find them, would it not add much to our understanding of the thwarted genius of Branwell to study these little figures?

I am ready to purchase them for the price of £5,000 sterling, or to reward suitably anyone leading me to the discovery of them.

Be assured that these soldiers would be entrusted to a museum, perhaps in Philadelphia or Boston, where they could be admired by all.

I remain, sir,

Your obedient servant,
SENECA D. BREWER, *Professor*"

"Now, isn't that going too far? I ask you, understanding the thwarted genius of Branwell Brontë by examining his wooden soldiers. Richest thing I've read in years. And as if they'd still be in existence, made of *wood*, you know."

The family had sat silent, except for Philip, who had laughed at the professor's name. Max and Jane gazed at each other and then looked quickly away.

Mrs. Morley spoke. "But, Rod, Maxy's are wooden and they've survived," she said. "They're nearly as old, I suppose."

"I know. I thought of Maxy's. It seemed a strange coincidence. But his were carefully wrapped up and put away, don't you see?" He began to eat his supper. "If the Brontës' had been carefully put away, they'd have been found at Haworth by now."

"Five thousand pounds!" Philip whistled.

"Scholarship gone mad," said Mr. Morley. "As if a wooden soldier, or even a set of wooden soldiers, could tell you anything!"

"But it's an interesting idea," Mrs. Morley said.

"What do you bet half the families in Yorkshire will suddenly find wooden soldiers in their attics?" their father said.

Max felt as if his food was choking him. Jane took frequent large gulps of water. Her cheeks were burning. Max was afraid somebody would notice.

11

The History of the Young Men

WHEN Max's mother came upstairs to tuck him in, she was carrying a large book which looked very learned. Max and Jane had had a hurried and rather frightened discussion in the bathroom. Max had said it was as good as proven whose the soldiers were. Jane had asked what would happen if this old professor found the right soldiers; would he take them to America? If so, they must be more careful than ever to be secret and to protect them. Max and Jane agreed that Butter Crashey and the rest would be stunned and terrified to be taken to America.

Max was lying in bed, wondering what was likely to happen next, following this strange turn of events. What worried him most was the extreme liveliness and activity of the Twelves. Anyone who went into the attic might see them at any minute. Their boldness had increased the more Max had got to know them, and their habit of freezing from fear had grown less and less. With this letter in the paper, his father and Philip and Mr. Howson and all the Howson family were likely to take an interest in them.

"Maxy! Please listen," said Mrs. Morley, sitting on the bed. "I thought you'd be interested, so I dug this out to read to you. It's a story Branwell Brontë wrote about his wooden soldiers, and it's called *The History of the Young Men*. He was only twelve when he wrote it."

"Where did you get it? Mr. Howson told us about it," said Max, trying to hide his excitement. "Call Janey too."

"Janey! Come and hear this." Jane came pattering in. "I remembered I had this volume of some of the stories the Brontës wrote when they were children. Look, Max, here's the list of the soldiers! *Look* at their names! One is Butter Crashey. Isn't that funny? Like your Butter!" Her finger ran down the list of soldiers. "And it gives their ages. There's even one called Stumps! Jane, he's hit on two of their names," she said, delighted. "Isn't he clever? Or had you heard about them at school?"

Max had twisted around in bed, and was reading the list, pointing at it. There they all were. Butter Crashey, Captain, 140, and all the others in order as he had got to know them. It was extraordinary. Max could hardly believe his eyes, but he remained quite calm. It was, in a way, no more than he had expected.

He grinned at his mother. "You see I'm as brilliant as those Brontës," he said, giggling. "Actually, Stumps has got stumpy legs, and Butter fell in the butter." Both these facts were true.

"Mummy," Jane said, "if this professor finds them, will he take them to America?"

"Oh yes, he's sure to. But there'll be an awful fuss from Haworth if he does. I'm afraid he's not likely to find them, though, because look what Branwell says. I've been reading it. Where is it? Here we are. . . . First he describes all his earlier sets of soldiers, and then he says. . . 'on June the fifth A.D. 1826, Papa procured me from Leeds another set [these were the Twelves] which I kept for two years, though two or three of them are in being at the time of my writing this [December fifteen A.D. 1830].' And then he goes on about some later sets. He was eight when he had them, Maxy. Your age. And he says by 1830 only two or three were left."

But Max and Jane, who were silent for a minute, knew better.

"Well," explained Max, for he knew there must be some explanation, "you see, *he* only had two or three, but that doesn't mean the others weren't somewhere. He could have just lost them around the place, and someone else could have picked them up and kept them."

"Yes," Jane said eagerly, "one of the girls easily could, you know, Mummy. Girls are much more careful than boys. They keep things longer, too, and they sort of can't bear to throw things away. I can't bear to throw away some of my baby things, even though I don't play with them any more." Jane was speaking very earnestly. "It's because girls love things longer."

Mrs. Morley wondered what Max would say to this.

She said, "I think that's true, Janey. What do you think, Max?"

"I think," Max said solemnly, "girls may love them for longer, I don't know, but they couldn't love them more. They absolutely couldn't love them more. More than I love the old soldiers now, say."

"So boys love things more strongly while they love them, and girls love them for longer, is that it? I think you may be about right. Anyway you must settle down, Max. It'll be very funny to see if anyone claims to find the Brontës' soldiers and gets the five thousand pounds."

"It's rather exciting, really, isn't it?" Jane said, watching her mother closely.

"Well, it could be if there were any way of knowing they were really the ones. But, you see, wooden soldiers are all much alike. If anyone has a set from about the right time, he could easily *say* they were the ones. But there's no proving it."

"That's what Daddy meant, then?" Jane said.

"Yes. He thinks someone will offer any old set to get five thousand pounds." She laughed, kissing Max. "I'll leave the book in case you want to read it in the morning. Good night, Maxy. Hurry up, Jane, it's late."

"Yes, I just want to tell Max something."

When their mother had gone, Jane said quickly, "Isn't it hard *not* to tell her? Shall we?"

"Not yet, no. We may have to though," Max replied.

He lay awake a long time, thinking of his soldiers. First he thought how strange it was that his mother had said wooden soldiers were all much alike, and how astonished and delighted she would be if she could see their faces go different and lively instead of blurred and wooden. He knew she would be delighted. He could imagine her face. She had often·said how amazing it was that God had made everybody absolutely different from every other body. Well, it was the same with the soldiers. Whoever had carved them had made them different, with great care, and it was his mother who had pointed this out. And then the four Genii, by imagining all these things, had added to it and had made them into real people. Max got up and carried the book to the window. He looked at the page his mother had left open, and his eye fell on one sentence:

> What is contained in this History is a statement of what myself, Charlotte, Emily and Anne really pretended did happen among the "Young Men" (that being the name we gave them) during the period of nearly six years. . . .

Max flopped back, leaving the book on the sill.

The Genii imagined them all so real, he thought to himself, that the Young Men still remember; they are still alive. Could this be what it was? He started to think of them in turn and which he loved best. He had told Jane and his mother that nobody could love anything more than he loved the Twelves. Now. And this was true. He wondered if this was another reason why they were so lively. Because he loved them and they trusted him. Nobody could help loving Butter Crashey. Max thought how Branwell and his sisters had had a special one each of them loved, and made a king. No wonder King Sneaky, Branwell's soldier, was the first to wake up with the drum, the first to make the others alive! No wonder. It was Branwell's game and Sneaky was his man, as Butter had said. It all fitted in. Max realized that his own special one was Stumps. He had lost him and found him again and guarded him and brought him back to the attic when he had so bravely climbed the creeper. He had had more to do with Stumps than with any of them so far. He wondered whose Jane's was, or would be.

But it was a mystery as to how they had reached this attic all together and none lost, when Branwell said only two or three were left. Perhaps it was what Jane suggested; one of the girls had been careful. Max suddenly felt a strange urge to go and ask Butter this at once. Surely Butter would know.

He scrambled out of bed again and tiptoed to the door. Jane had long since settled down. His mother and father and Philip must still be downstairs, though Philip would soon be coming up. It was safe. Max crept up the attic stairs, and then saw with a shock that the door was open and the light was on.

Philip was kneeling on the floor by the canoe, picking up the Twelves one by one, turning them over, looking at them as if they were what he thought they were, simply pieces of wood.

Max had a very quick temper. Now he felt a huge, hot wave of rage coming up into his throat from his heart, ready to drown him.

"Put my soldiers down. They're not yours! I haven't said you could touch them," he said in a hoarse, choking voice. "Put them down!" he

112

screamed, with his fists clenched and his teeth grinding together as Philip turned around in amazement. "Put them down. You'll hurt them. You'll break them. Who said you could touch them?"

"All right, all right. I'm only *looking* at them. I won't hurt them. It's really interesting, after what that old professor says. Did you arrange them all with their oars balanced in the canoe? Anyway, who said you could borrow my balsa?" Philip added, seizing on this advantage. He collected Butter and Stumps and Sneaky and Cheeky and Gravey from his knee, and tossed them, head first, higgledy-piggledy, back into the boat where they lay sprawled with all the others, who had evidently been treated similarly. The oars had fallen in every direction.

The thing in Max's heart burst. "You're not to throw them around!" he screamed. He dived at Philip, who was barely up from the ground. He beat him with his knuckles. He kicked him. He bit him. He scratched him. But Philip was much older and much stronger (he was fourteen) and soon mastered Max, trying hard to keep his own temper.

"Now you'll be sorry," he breathed, losing it as Max kicked. He flung Max onto the attic floor hard and went out, slamming the door.

"You've hurt them! You've killed them!" Max sobbed and he lay on the floor a long time, wanting to kill Philip, and crying because he couldn't stop crying. It was all spoiled. They would be frozen again. They might even be broken. He hardly dared to look.

He sat up at last, feeling as weak and wretched as anyone does who has lost his temper, and his eyes

113

were so swollen he could hardly see through them. He rubbed them. He heard a familiar whispery, whisking noise. He peered at the canoe anxiously.

The Twelves were sitting in an orderly fashion,

"Goodbye, Noble Crashey!"

BERNARDA
BRYSON

along the bottom, engaged in earnest conversation. They were evidently discussing what had happened. They seemed very excited and no one was hurt. Sneaky was on his feet, waving his arms around as if he were talking at a public meeting.

Max put out his hand and took Butter Crashey gently from the bow of the boat.

"Are you hurt, Oh Patriarch?" he said, sniffing, but comforted to feel Butter's lizard body in his fingers.

"An immense monster seized upon us all in turn," Butter said, "and after turning us around as if we were sacks of coal or potatoes, tossed us through the air without ceremony. We, not recognizing him, remained frozen."

"I know. I saw. I was afraid you were hurt," Max whispered.

"Hurt?" questioned Butter with dignity. "We who have been through such perils? Sailing in the *Invincible* (a deal better than this boat we are reduced to), conquering the Ashanti, carving out our kingdom, building our cities?"

Max smiled and nodded.

"Also," said the patriarch, "have you forgotten the secret process of being made alive? We, whom the four Genii constantly made alive and protected? We, who were collected from the four corners where we were scattered in old age, and were banded together again, indestructible, the Twelves, the Young Men? Hurt?" he demanded, drawing himself up proudly in Max's hand and at the same time stumbling slightly in the rut between Maxy's fingers.

"Oh, Butter Crashey," said Max, careful not to

115

smile, "of course not. I'm sorry I insulted you." And then he remembered the question he had come to ask, and realized it was partly answered. "Who collected you from the four corners? One of the female Genii?"

"That I cannot say, for it is lost in the mists of antiquity," said the patriarch. He shook his head.

Max put Butter gently back among the chattering Twelves, and went to bed, worn out with his feelings.

12

The Reward

THE book which contained the story of the Young Men was gone when Max woke up. He supposed his mother must have come in and taken it after he was asleep, and had forgotten to put it back.

Actually, Philip had taken it after he had left Max crying in the attic. Now he was sitting up in bed, continuing to read the story and everything else in the volume which concerned the wooden soldiers the professor was looking for. Philip had studied Max's soldiers with a detailed and scientific interest such as he applied to his work at school. He had already noticed, in the shoe box where Max kept them, a few of the round stands that balanced the soldiers, and now he had found Branwell's own description of what the soldiers looked like, including those round stands which Branwell referred to as their one shoe. "This shoe, for each man wore only one, was like a round flat cake with two holes in the middle into which his feet were inserted as in a stocks," Branwell had written. And at the bottom of the page in a footnote he had added: "The curious shoe was the little stand which each soldier had to keep him from falling." Philip also thought Branwell's description of what they wore tallied with Max's soldiers: "A high black cap with several hieroglyphical figures on it." But these, Philip thought, would naturally be rubbed off by now. "Their coat, or rather jacket, was shaped after the manner of a sailor's and was in color a light scarlet. They also wore light pantaloons of the same color." There wasn't much color left now, but they certainly had been scarlet. Philip, in his time, had been just as crazy about soldiers as Max was, and he couldn't help a feeling of excitement that here might be the very ones this famous Branwell had written about. He read backward and forward in the book. He found Charlotte's description of how each girl seized a soldier from Branwell's new box, named him, and called him hers. He found the part where Branwell said that two or three (only) were still around. But like Max, this didn't worry him. Someone else could have collected and preserved what Branwell had lost or broken.

Now, if it could be proven they were the ones, wasn't Max due for five thousand pounds? Philip was a practical boy and he liked money. He had been going to suggest to Maxy that he would help him write the letter to the professor describing his find, for a small percentage to be paid when Max had received his five thousand. But Max had been in such a devilish temper that Philip could say nothing of this plan. And also Philip had an idea that Max was so enchanted with these soldiers that he might not *want* to sell them. Otherwise, why had he flown into such a rage at Philip's touching them? Of course Philip knew there was a kind of unwritten law in the family about not playing with each other's things without asking. He supposed he should have asked, and he didn't quite know why he hadn't, except that Max was in bed and his curiosity overcame him.

When Philip came to the list of soldiers and reread it carefully, noticing Butter Crashey was one hundred and forty, he did think it was odd. Max could have heard the *name* somehow or made it up in the way he said when the soldier fell in the butter. But that he should also be one hundred and forty. . . . Perhaps Max had got hold of this book and read the list. Or someone at school had told them about the Brontë soldiers. That was more likely. The same reasons could account for Stumps, whose name he saw farther down. Max had remembered some of the names he had been told and used them. But in that case, if he knew about the Brontë soldiers, why hadn't he said so at Mr. Howson's? And again, when his father read the professor's letter?

Philip remembered that Max had blushed and been absolutely silent when Mr. Rochester told him about the soldiers. Did Max know these were the Brontës' soldiers? But how could he know? Anyway, Max knew more than he was saying, Philip decided.

Either he had to work on his own and write to this Seneca D. Brewer himself in secret, or he had to ingratiate himself with Max and be let into whatever it was Max knew. (He had an idea Jane was in it.)

119

To get Max to let him into it was difficult when he had thrown his brother onto the attic floor as hard as he could.

Could it be done through Janey? This was possible. Meanwhile, *what* did Max know? There really was no proving these were the very soldiers. There never would be, as his father had said, and they hadn't even been found at Haworth.

But did that matter? If this professor wanted to think they were, why not let him? If he was really silly enough to pay five thousand pounds for some old wooden soldiers, he would probably be willing to come all the way from America to look at the ones Max had.

No, Philip decided, the chance was much too good to be lost, and he had better get in first before anyone else offered their soldiers. He slammed the book shut and swung out of bed with his mind made up. He returned the volume to Max's room while Max was out, and as soon as breakfast was over he bicycled to the postoffice, purchased an airmail envelope, and wrote a suitable letter to Professor Seneca D. Brewer.

From this it can be seen that Philip was a clear-sighted boy with keenness and determination, and when he did this he was thinking quite honestly how good it would be for Max (to say nothing of the rest of them, who might share a little in his fortune) to get the reward. Even if Max now thought that he cared more for the soldiers than the money, he wouldn't still think so in a few years' time.

But Philip didn't know the whole story as yet.

Up in Max's bedroom, Max was telling Jane of last

night's adventure. The book lay between them on the bed, and they meant to read it later.

"And I'd just like to cut all the strings in his tennis racket or puncture his bike tires," Max finished venomously, still feeling angry over Philip's behavior.

"Well look, Max, the chief thing is that Butter and the others weren't *hurt*," Jane said. "But I *do* think we ought to protect them more."

"So do I. Butter said that since they didn't recognize the monster, they all remained frozen. But will they always be quick enough to do that? Do you think I ought to warn Butter to tell them to? Supposing Mummy and Daddy ask to see them again because of this old professor's letter? And what if someone goes into the attic and they're doing things?"

"Yes, or looks through the keyhole while we're in there. Max, do you think Philip's going to do anything?"

"What could he do?"

"He could write to that professor, couldn't he, and tell him about your soldiers?"

"But he'd ask Daddy and Mummy first, wouldn't he?" Max said, horrified.

Jane looked doubtful.

"We *could* hide them somewhere if we had to," she said.

This idea comforted Max, and he felt very glad that he had Jane to help him.

They went up to the attic, found that the door had a rusty bolt inside (perhaps it had once been a bedroom), and made this work by using the bicycle oil.

Jane also found a small piece of wood to fill up the keyhole from inside. There was no key.

With these precautions taken, they felt happier.

"Max," Jane said, turning to an idea she had thought of last night in bed, "may I make them a feast?"

Max stared at her. It sounded suspiciously like a doll's teaparty.

"But, Jane, you can't *play* with them like that," he protested.

"I didn't mean play with them," she said. "I only meant put it all out and see if they like it—"

"You can't sit them up or anything. They'd probably be offended," he explained.

"I know. I wasn't going to. But you fed them, you said so, when they were on the kitchen table. After all, you've done lots of things with them, seeing them get downstairs and all that, and I haven't done anything."

Jane, being a girl, was really perhaps more interested in feeding the Twelves than seeing them on parade.

"Oh, all right. It can't hurt to set it out, I suppose," Max said. "I know. I'll make a great table, like at a banquet, while you get the things."

"Yes," Jane said, and she slipped out and hurried downstairs.

Max got his bricks and laid some in a row. Over these he put an old Monopoly board folded up. Around this imposing table he put more bricks, enough to seat the Young Men. At the head of the table he built a more splendid seat than the others,

122

higher and with a back and arms. This he intended for the patriarch.

"But," Max muttered, "I wouldn't be surprised if one of those four kings doesn't swipe it."

So he put four second-best seats on each side of the patriarch, two on a side. These had backs but no arms. They were meant for the kings. The seats beyond them on each side were simply single bricks with no backs or arms and were meant for the other soldiers.

I hope they'll know what I mean, Max said to himself. All this took a good deal of fiddling to find the right-sized bricks, and when Jane came back, Max had only just finished.

"That's super," she whispered. She quickly began to set the table with the tiny brass plates she had kept from her dollhouse days. At either end she put a brass candlestick, and between these, small plates, gleaming at the edges, filled with bread crumbs, cake crumbs, cooky crumbs, dried-up coconut, raisins and silver sprinkles. These plates were milk bottle tops. By each man's own plate she put a tiny wineglass. Finally, quite aware that the Twelves would expect strong drink and not tea, she put a decanter filled with a rich red drink at each end.

Max was delighted. Imagine Jane having kept all the wineglasses and decanters unbroken! She had had them years ago. He had broken the stem from one, but his mother had carefully glued it back. It was true, what Jane said about girls being careful with their things.

When the feast was spread, the Genie Janeii retired

modestly to the other end of the attic and waited. Max picked up the patriarch, who all this time had sat motionless with the others in the canoe.

"The Genii have spread you a table in the wilderness," he said. "Partake if you choose." As he said it he thought of the Twenty-Third Psalm, though he couldn't quite think why. It seemed a suitable way of inviting Butter Crashey, who at once bowed and showed every sign of pleasure. Max put him back and sat on the Ashanti stool.

The Twelves weren't long in accepting the invitation. They fixed a balsa-wood gangplank and scrambled or slid down it, according to taste, running for seats at the table as if they hadn't seen a banquet for years, which was indeed the case. The younger members—notably the midshipmen Crackey, Tracky and Monkey—elbowed and pushed and squealed with excitement. The more stalwart warriors took their middle places with more ceremony, while the four kings and the patriarch himself walked from the boat in a solemn procession. Sneaky strutted with such an air of conceited haughtiness and yawned with such a bored flourish of his hand to his mouth that it made Max laugh. But he couldn't help noticing that their walk became brisk as they neared their places.

They ate, drank, talked, choked, laughed, toasted, slapped each other on the back and grew very merry as befitted such gallant Young Men.

Bravey, indeed, so far forgot himself as to leap up on his seat, jump wildly in the air, and wave his arms as he sang in a loud voice:

"Cannikin clink
Drink, boys, drink,
Drink, drink,
Cannikin clink."

This song, evidently well known to the others, caused immense excitement. The decanters were seized and passed around, glasses clinked, more than one Young Man followed Bravey's example and stood up on his chair. Sneaky danced so wildly and jumped so high in the air that it seemed doubtful to Max whether he would land on the seat again, and more likely that the table would be upset and Jane's wine-glasses broken beyond repair. The patriarch, however, called them to order, and the wild junketing gave place to brave stories and loud laughter. When not a crumb was left, not a drop of ruby-red liquid, and when several were showing distinct signs of inebriation, the patriarch arose.

Max leaned forward eagerly to hear what he would say, and Jane crawled a little nearer.

"Beware, Young Men, of all monsters such as he who seized upon us recently. Show no signs of life to any but the two Genii you know. This warning came to me from the present chief Genie. An unknown danger threatens the Twelves." The patriarch held up his hands and took his splendid seat again. The bell rang for lunch. Max and Jane tiptoed from the attic.

"When did you warn Butter?" she said. "About Philip?"

"I didn't. Only in my mind. I was going to," Max

125

said, "but he seems to know. He said it to me once. He said that the chief Genie said, 'Revere this man Crashey, he is entrusted with secrets which you can never know.'"

"So we needn't worry too much," Jane said, "only keep our eyes open."

At lunch, their father had a newspaper by his plate. "I said that professor's letter would raise a fuss." He laughed. "Listen to this one:

"SIR,
    In the unlikely event of the set of Brontë soldiers to which Professor Seneca D. Brewer refers in his letter coming to light, it is to be hoped that the owner or finder will know his local, no, his national duty, and will offer them to the Brontë Museum. This is their rightful home, and we in this part of Yorkshire are their rightful guardians. It would be monstrous if this unexpected remnant of the Brontë heritage should cross the Atlantic.
    I remain, sir, etc., etc.

"He's so upset, and they're not even found yet," said Mr. Morley, laughing.

"I wonder if the museum will get into this," said Mrs. Morley.

"Will they offer to pay the five thousand pounds for them instead of letting them go?" asked Jane.

"There's no knowing," her father said. "Maxy, shall we write to the old professor and say you have them?" he suggested, half teasing. "And get the five thousand pounds?"

Max's face went white. He swallowed.

"No," he said fiercely. "They're mine. I found them. I don't want five thousand pounds! You *can't!*"

126

13

The Battle of Atticum

IN the next few days Max and Jane spent more time with the Twelves than with the rest of the family. For one thing, the fine hot weather had broken. Mrs. Morley, still busy with all the details of settling into the new house, hardly noticed how much they were in the attic. For another, Jane had become as enslaved to the Young Men as Max, but in a rather different way. It was Jane who first said that they should pick up and speak to each Young Man, that they should get to know them separately. For a third, all the fuss about the American professor seemed to have died down; their father had said no more, and Philip had been particularly nice to Max, as if he were trying to make up for the fight in the attic.

It was Jane who noticed that Crackey, aged five, had indeed—in his wooden state—a crack in the back of his head beneath his hat.

"How did you get that, Crackey?" Jane whispered.

"Hit by a cannon ball and never healed up," replied Crackey promptly and proudly.

Hit by a cannon ball and never healed up!

And it was Jane who saw that Tracky, aged ten, was forever following people around and tracking them down. When he managed to take them by surprise, he would fling his arms around them and shout "Got you!" Very much as Max sometimes did. Jane also noticed that Tracky was a particular pest to sober King Parry. The two were evidently enemies of long standing, and she wondered what old quarrel lay behind it.

128

Jane observed, too, how like a tiny ape's was the bright-eyed, snubby face of Monkey. He behaved like a monkey, climbing everything he could find—something he must have learned when he was a midshipman on the *Invincible*.

"And you know, Jane," Max said, "they're all horrid to poor old Gravey. I know he's gloomy and never smiles, but whenever he opens his mouth they sneer at him."

"Yes, and he often falls over because he's either nervous or he's absent-minded or something, and then they all laugh," she added, for she had seen this too.

"I don't wonder he's sour, as Branwell says in the story, do you? Maybe if you were to spoil him a little, he'd feel better," Max suggested.

As for the volatile Sneaky, he was often seen playing tricks on the others, sneaking up on them, tripping them, blowing down their necks and then looking the other way, and generally behaving in a most unkingly fashion. Then he would suddenly go into a mood and look haughty and dark and hide in some corner by himself and sneer at anyone who came to talk to him, and make bitter remarks about his fate. He was certainly, as Jane said, a strange mixture.

The other two kings, Parry and Ross, were more straightforward and dignified but very clever. Parry was tall and spare, Ross was shorter and broader, and seemed the most open in the way he behaved. It was often these two who led the others on climbing expeditions in the attic. Over mountains of books, up to the plateaus of trunks and furniture they went, look-ing down from these dizzy heights to piles of folded curtains below. They would cross a glacier (a mirror not yet in use) and from there jump into a soft snow-drift of spare blankets. When they did these things, Max and Jane had to watch them carefully lest one should get left behind and lost.

One morning the telegraph boy came whistling up to the Morley's door and knocked loudly. Philip, who had been lurking around the house the last day or two almost as if he were expecting something of the kind, darted out of the living room, rushed to the door, and signed for a cablegram.

He began to open it at once, telling the boy there wouldn't be an answer.

"How do you know it's for you?" Jane asked, on her way to do an errand for her mother.

"Because it says so," Philip growled, disappearing again.

Now that he had done it—now that his letter had reached the professor and the professor had answered —Philip felt worried and uneasy. How was he to tell Max? How was he to persuade Max that this was all for his good? What would his mother and father say? And what would all those outraged people who wrote to the paper say if the soldiers left England? Philip read the message again:

FLYING TO ENGLAND FIFTEENTH TO INSPECT WOODEN SOLDIERS.
BREWER

Philip chewed his knuckles, and then flicked his

130

fingers, standing first on one foot and then on the other.

Would Seneca D. Brewer expect to be entertained by Mrs. Morley? And what would Mrs. Morley think about this?

Philip often referred to his mother as Mrs. Morley. It was a kind of joke he used when he needed anything very badly or had something to confess. Now he wandered out to the kitchen, looking vacant on purpose.

"Mrs. Morley," he said.

"Hullo, darling, what do you want?" she asked at once.

Philip handed her the cablegram.

"What's this?" she said, taking it with a floury hand. "Philip, do you mean you wrote to him?"

Philip nodded, still looking vacant, his eyes fixed on a far corner of the ceiling.

"But what did you tell him?"

"Just how Max had found the soldiers and that they go with the ones in *The History of the Young Men*."

"But does Max know? Does he agree? You heard what he said to Daddy."

"He doesn't know."

"Well, Philip, whatever made you do it, when you heard what Max said?" she asked.

"I'd already done it."

His mother was silent, for she couldn't help admiring his prompt efficiency. She supposed he had compared the soldiers with the description in the book. On the other hand, it was no joke to bring a professor

131

flying over the Atlantic, only to find a small boy who wouldn't part with some wooden soldiers. She said so.

"I know," Philip said gloomily, "but surely he'll listen to reason. After all, five thousand pounds!"

"Phil, you know the kind of a boy Max is. Money means nothing to him yet. Why should it? Also, how can anyone possibly tell?" she said crossly. "There's no proof they're the ones; such things were made by the thousands. How can we take all that money from a crazy scholar who's let an idea run away with him?"

"That's his worry. But you know what Max calls them? Don't you remember that first day, he called them the Twelves? And you said what is the twelves? I remember distinctly. And have you forgotten that one is Butter, aged one hundred and forty, and one is Stumps? It's all in that book, you know. How did Max *know*?"

"Well, he and Jane have been reading the book."

"Mrs. Morley," Philip said, in some exasperation, "it was all *before* you produced the book. You wouldn't make a good detective. Max knows something—more than he's saying."

"What *do* you mean, Philip? How could he? He brought that old roll of rags with them inside right down, quite openly, to show us all."

"Just the same, I swear he's got some clue that those soldiers belonged to the Brontës. Well, what shall I do?" he asked appealingly, as if he were Max's age again.

"You must go up and tell him what you've done. You've got yourself into it, Phil. You must simply go and tell him, and see what he thinks. He may be

132

willing to part with them. You must stop this poor man from coming if he's not. But you're not to bully and upset Max, now."

Philip went slowly upstairs, working out a plan of campaign as carefully as a general works out a battle.

Meanwhile Max was alone in the attic, absorbed in another battle. He had set out the chessmen, in a cohort, as if they were a rival army, for he had just read in Branwell's story how he had let the Twelves fight some cannibal ninepins. Sure enough, the Young Men had at once taken them for an army and had prepared for battle. The Duke of Wellington, Bravey, Ross and Parry had dragged Max's bag of marbles across the attic floor, and every man was seizing on these glittering cannon balls and bowling them, with a noise like small thunder, across the attic floor at the chessmen. Whenever a man was hit, there was a howl of glee, and if he was hit three times, he was ignominiously pushed from the field. Tracky was acting as ball boy, returning the cannon which missed; Monkey was beating the Ashanti drum with the balsa wood; the Duke was standing on a pedestal made of two checkers, the flag planted beside him, urging his men on. The best shots were undoubtedly Stumps, Cheeky, Parry and Ross. Sneaky was too excited to aim straight, but Gravey was extremely good as he kept his eye on the balls and never wavered or took time off to ask the rest to admire him.

Meanwhile Butter had wanted to be picked up, and now he surveyed the battle of Atticum, as Max called it, from Max's hand, his two arms held aloft like

133

Moses in the Bible, as if he were holding up the good cause of the Twelves.

Max heard Philip's step, thought the attic door was bolted, remembered Jane had gone out, and sprang to his feet too late.

The attic door was opened even as Max hissed "monster!" Butter Crashey was still waving his arms wildly as Philip came in, and in a quick instinctive movement to hide him, Max plunged him into his pocket, keeping his fingers on him.

The battle had frozen. Some soldiers feigned dead. One solitary marble went rumbling away past Monkey toward the drum into the far corner of the attic.

"Hullo," Philip said pleasantly.

"Hullo," said Max cautiously. He sat down on the Ashanti stool, his hand gently around Butter Crashey in his pocket.

"Maxy," Philip began, and as he spoke he picked up—who was it?—Max's darling Stumps (as Jane called him). He held him with great care and consideration, however, looking at him off and on.

"You know that professor," he went on, "who wrote to the paper about the soldiers?"

"Yes," said Max. And his heart gave a great, uncontrolled *wumph*, like the noise of the drum.

"Well, you don't think it would hurt, do you, for him to come and see these soldiers? Just to look at them and see if he thinks they're the ones he wants?" Philip coaxed.

"I don't care whether he wants them or not," Max replied, going right to the point. "He's not going to have them, so what's the use of his coming to see them?"

"But if they are the right ones," Philip went on, "he'll give you five thousand pounds for them. Think how useful that would be! Max, you'll be able to get all sorts of things you want. And after all, if he takes them to America, they'll be very well looked after. They have the most marvellous museums and collections and things in America. They can't come to any harm."

"They're not going to America," Max said, "because I'm not selling them."

"Well, it's not really selling, it's a kind of reward for finding them. You know, you won't want to play with them in a few more years, I promise you."

"I don't play with them now," said Max with dignity.

Philip smiled. "Anyway, if it once gets known you've got them, they'll want them at Haworth at the Brontë Museum. You won't be allowed to keep them here. I bet Mummy and Daddy won't let you. Haworth is where they used to be, if they really are Branwell's. The Genie Brannii," he added. "Good, isn't it, that story?"

"Mummy said," Max replied stubbornly, "that nobody could possibly prove they're the ones, so the museum can't take them."

Philip was silent a moment.

"But *you* think they are, don't you?" he asked next, trying a different approach.

Max held onto Butter rather tightly and said nothing. His eyes were on Stumps, who was being waved through the air quite a bit; enough to make him faint or be sick, Max thought. He hoped Stumps was safely frozen.

"You *do*, don't you, Maxy?"

Still Max said nothing.

"I wonder why," Philip said, trying to draw him out. "Anyway," he said briskly, feeling slightly ashamed because he was up against something he didn't understand, "this professor's coming. Just to see them. It can't hurt."

"How does he know I've got them?" Max said, unable to believe what was obvious.

"Because I told him," leered Philip, teasing. He leered because now he really was ashamed, feeling Max's seriousness and distress.

"But I told Daddy not to. I said I didn't want him to write," Max said in the utmost consternation.

"I wrote before you ever said that," Philip said.

"You are a beast!"

Philip didn't look at him, for he was afraid his eyes were full of tears.

"But I thought you'd be pleased to get the money when you'd thought it over," Philip said. "So I just did it. Look, this is what he says."

Max read the cable.

"I'm sorry you're mad," Philip said, putting on a slightly hurt voice. "I thought you'd be pleased."

"But you don't understand," Max said helplessly, stroking Butter with one finger. He held out the other hand and took Stumps from his brother. Then he turned away and went over to the open attic window.

He put Stumps on the sill and looked out across the moors.

"Oh well," Philip said, and shrugged his shoulders. "You can always say no, if you're so silly." And he went out, relieved that it was over.

14

Gone

EACH morning Mr. Morley would seize the newspaper and turn to the correspondence to see if there
were any more letters about the soldiers. There was a
lull after the first day or two, and then they started
again.

"Now, that's exactly what I think," their father
said with satisfaction, reading a letter. "It's what I
said, you remember." Everybody likes having his own
opinion backed up and Mr. Morley sounded very
pleased.

"What is?" asked Philip.

"Read it, Daddy," Jane urged. "Is it a new one
about the soldiers?"

"Yes. 'Sir, [read her father, crackling the paper in
his square brown hands], It is surely infantile to suppose that the cause of serious literary criticism, or
even of serious biography, however psychologically
slanted, can possibly be furthered by the examination

of some wooden toys of a kind made by the thousands and played with in their childhood by the Brontë family. What they imagined and wrote about these soldiers is perhaps valuable and certainly revealing. Much of it is published and available. To think the toys themselves would be illuminating is only sentimental. I remain,' and so forth. I hope Seneca D. Brewer reads that," he finished.

Max sat up with a jerk and his eyes glittered as he looked at Jane. There were a great many hard words in the letter, yet he thought he got the sense of it. The soldiers, being wooden and like many others, couldn't tell anybody anything. How little these people knew about the venerable Crashey, the Duke of Wellington, dear Stumps, lively Sneaky, bold Cheeky, gloomy Gravey, hard-drinking Bravey, Monkey and the other midshipmen! He looked at his father, smiling. Mr. Morley thought that Max was pleased because the letter meant that his soldiers were in less danger of being pursued and put in a museum.

He winked and said, "That'll settle Seneca, eh, Max?"

Then a silence fell around the table, because Mr. Morley was the only one who didn't yet know that the professor was about to fly the Atlantic and bear down on them. Mr. Morley saw his family exchange glances.

"Go on, Philip," his mother said, "Tell."

"What?" said Philip's father, startled.

"Seneca's coming," Philip said, enjoying the sensation he was causing. He took the cablegram from his pocket and pushed it toward his father.

139

"Philip, you are a young idiot!" Mr. Morley said crossly when he realized what it meant.

"Daddy, *you* suggested writing yourself. Actually I'd already done it," Philip said, his voice rising high with injury and protest, "but you know you did."

"What are we going to do?" Mr. Morley asked his wife.

"I don't know," she said resignedly. "Maxy won't part with them. There's no proving they're the ones. The whole thing is ridiculous. But it's not our fault. The man must have money to burn. I've told Philip he should stop him."

"Philip, you must have given him the impression they're the Brontë soldiers, if he's willing to fly to see them," Mr. Morley said gloomily, turning to the paper again for consolation. "Here's another letter, all about the horrors of war and how boys shouldn't be allowed to play with soldiers. That would be from one of the Friends."

Yorkshire has a good number of Friends, or Quakers, a religious group which strongly disapproves of anything to do with war. They will never be soldiers or fight in any way; they will only help the victims. Should anything which glorifies war, asked this ardent Friend—even a set of wooden soldiers which inspired the imaginations of the four Brontës—be allowed to be so important as to cause a hue and cry and the offer of a huge reward? Give your five thousand pounds, he told the professor sternly, to the refugees, the guiltless victims of the last terrible war and those oppressions which followed it.

"Well, I must say I agree with him," said their mother.

"There'll be answers to both of those, I imagine," Mr. Morley said.

It wasn't only through the newspaper that the interest in the Brontë soldiers grew. It soon became clear that people in the neighborhood were beginning to know of the Morleys' possible part in the affair.

Bill, for instance, Mr. Morley's hired man, was curious. "It's queer what it says in the paper about the toy soldiers that Brontë boy had. Think it's your boy who's found them?"

Mr. Morley was taken by surprise and hedged. "But there can't be any proof whatever that any soldiers found here have anything to do with the Brontës, Bill. How could there be?"

And he thought to himself, How did Bill know? Has Max told him?

"But folks is saying that some professor's comin' over here all the way from America, just to see them."

Mr. Morley realized then that it might have leaked out about the cable, and no wonder it had caused talk. Why shouldn't the village people be interested? They read their newspaper, like everyone else.

The baker, coming up to the kitchen door, said cheerfully to Mrs. Morley, "Now, ma'am, it beats all, what they say these here wooden soldiers'll fetch. My, but I wouldn't mind finding them myself, I can tell you that!"

Mrs. Morley couldn't tell from this whether he knew of Max's find or whether he had only read the

141

paper, so she just said that she expected the fuss would die down soon.

But Jane, who had overheard both conversations and had carefully said nothing, quickly ran up to the attic, where Max was.

"Angria," she whispered through the keyhole, tapping three times. This was their password. They had found out from the book that the name which Branwell and Charlotte Brontë later gave to their imaginary country of the Young Men was Angria. "Instead of Africa, I suppose," Jane had said. So they had decided to use it for a password.

Max unbolted the door and Jane slipped inside.

"Maxy," she began anxiously, "everyone seems to know about them. Bill's just told Daddy that he hears you may be the lucky finder. And the baker said something about them to Mummy—"

Max interrupted her.

"Who told Bill? Philip?"

"I asked Mummy that. She says she thinks it may be because of the cable arriving. Where are they all anyway?" she whispered.

"They've gone on a climbing trip. Over Daddy's knapsack. Can you see? Ross used the cord to pull himself up, and now they're all doing it. Look."

Jane looked and saw a line of the Young Men pulling themselves up the steep gray wrinkled slopes of the knapsack by the cord which hung from its neck. Ross, Sneaky and the Duke had reached the top, jumped over the edge, and were peering out as if it were a great crater. The knapsack was full of camping stuff and there was a ground sheet folded at the top.

"They're so clever," she said.

"Yes. *And* brave," added Max. "After all, it might be a volcano for all they probably know."

"Maxy, what *are* we going to do when this professor arrives?" Jane said when they had watched the mountaineers a little longer. Gravey had just stumbled over a slippery bulge and was swinging by the rope. A wave of thin jeering laughter could be heard from the slope, and even the Duke—at the edge of the crater—was smiling. As for Sneaky, he was doubled up with laughter.

"Never mind, Gravey darling," Jane said in a gentle whisper. "The Genii love and protect you."

Gravey renewed his foothold and climbed on, his sad face full of determination.

"I don't know about the professor. That's what I've been trying to think out, Jane. I want Mummy to stop him from coming. And the only thing I can think of is to let her into the secret."

"What I'm afraid of is that if we tell a grownup, they'll say it can't be true, and the Twelves will freeze forever."

"I know, that's what I thought. It would have to be a special kind of a person who understood. Surely if they saw them alive they couldn't say it wasn't true. And then they'd help us protect them."

"Yes. Mummy would know how to put everyone off."

"Or should we just hide them, Jane? Put them somewhere away from here, in their box?"

"Max, they'd *hate* it!"

Together they wondered how they could possibly explain to Butter Crashey and the others that for the time being they must be buried alive again.

"Of course they'd freeze then all right," Max said.

"Yes. And they might never come back to life," Jane added.

"We could explain that it wouldn't be any worse than being under the floorboard. And we'd rescue them again when it was safe. I wonder if the Howsons would mind if we used their cave right behind the house? Nobody would look there," Max suggested.

"Do we want to tell the Howsons? Maxy, what about Mr. Howson, Mr. Rochester?" Jane said suddenly. "*He'd* be interested. He'd believe in them and help us!"

Max nodded. He had promised to show Mr. Howson the soldiers. Mr. Howson was a brontyfan and knew all about the Young Men.

"I bet he's been reading the letters in the newspaper," Max said.

At this minute they heard their mother's step on the stair and her voice calling.

"Maxy! Jane! Are you in the attic?"

"Yes," they answered, springing up.

"Well, Max, there's a reporter calling from the paper, asking about the soldiers. Open the door, darling, I don't want to have to shout. Why do you keep the door locked?" Mrs. Morley, not unnaturally impatient, wiggled the handle.

"I'm coming out," Max said hastily, and did.

144

"This man wants to know whether it's true that one of my sons has found some soldiers like the Brontë ones. And may he come and interview the finder and photograph him with his find?"

"It's all those letters." Max scowled. "Who *told* them?"

"Darling, I don't know. What am I to say? He's on the phone."

"Did you tell him it was true?" Max demanded.

"No. I said I wondered how he'd heard that, and that I'd come and ask you."

Max looked at his mother gratefully.

"Well, say *no*, Mummy," he ordered.

"You won't give an interview? Doesn't it sound grand? And what about photographing the soldiers?"

"No, no, no," Max said in terror. "They don't want to be in the paper and I don't either, Mummy."

Mrs. Morley thought how different Max was from other boys who might like being in the newspapers. And again she wondered at his fierce and secret attachment to these soldiers.

"I'm afraid they'll make up a story if we don't give them one. But I'll just say no and hang up," she said. "Is Janey there?"

"Yes. Thank you, Mummy," Max said. "I think Phil's a beast. It's all his fault about the cable," he blurted out.

"It's all a lot of nonsense in my opinion," she said. She wanted to ask Max what there was about these soldiers. "They don't want to be in the paper," he had said. But she remembered the reporter still on the telephone and hurried downstairs.

"Jane," Max said, going back into the attic, "did you hear? It's getting *dangerous*!"

"Yes, I did." Jane nodded.

That afternoon the reporter didn't bother to phone again. He simply came. Jane and Max stampeded to the attic and bolted the door. They heard their mother repeat over and over that she had nothing to say. Not long after this Mr. Howson telephoned Mr. Morley, saying he was so interested to read all this in the paper and he couldn't help connecting it with Max's soldiers and could he possibly come and see them tomorrow? Mr. Morley naturally said yes.

On the way to bed Jane and Max decided that they would let Mr. Howson see the Twelves. If the time seemed right, they would warn Butter Crashey and present the noble patriarch, lively and wise, to the parson, and ask for his advice as an elder Genie.

When they had decided this, they felt happier. Max said that, after all, they could always tell their mother too. She had been marvelous with the reporter.

The next morning when they went up to get the Young Men ready in ranks for inspection, not a soldier was in sight.

"Oh, they've mountaineered somewhere," Max said, beginning to search.

"Yes, I guess so," Jane answered, joining in.

They searched high, they searched low, under, inside, back of beyond. They searched more and more quickly and loudly, bumping into each other, with fear growing inside them.

"Jane! In the knapsack!"

"No. Max, in that roll of carpet!"

"No. In their box?"

"No. Max, under their old floorboard?"

Max dived for the squeaky board, scrabbled frantically at it, and lifted it up. Empty. He put his hands right in as far as they would go. Dirt and cobwebs.

"No!" Max was almost crying and Jane was pale.

"They've gone!" she said at last, clutching her hands over her chest.

Lost? Not lost in the attic. They had searched. And the door had been safely shut at night. Stolen?

The window was open. They often had it open and seldom bothered to shut it unless it rained. It was wide open this morning. Had the Twelves strayed? Who could tell?

Max flopped over the Ashanti stool. "We haven't protected them," he sobbed. "We've let them be taken. What will happen to them?"

15

Where?

"MAX! Jane!" Mrs. Morley called up the attic stairs. "Can you bring the soldiers down or must Mr. Howson climb up?"

"Maxy!" Jane said, shaking his shoulder gently. "He's here. Mr. Howson. Stop crying, Max. Coming, Mummy," she called from the door.

But she knew what Max was thinking. He was thinking how puzzled and hurt the patriarch and the Duke and the others would be to be treated as wooden with no thoughts or feelings. She was thinking the same thing herself. She was wondering about Crackey, aged five, and Monkey and poor melancholy Gravey, whose spirits she always had to encourage by loving him especially. Who had taken them? Who was turning them over now and looking at them and putting them headfirst into a box somewhere?

"Max, we'll have to go. Come on," she said, going to the attic door.

"Stumps sings songs," remarked Max miserably,

getting up and rubbing at his eyes. The thought of Stumps' brave climb made his tears start again.

Side by side they went down the attic stairs, slowly and soberly. Max ran his hands down the bannisters.

"Their string," he sniffed, noticing it and remembering the adventurous descent.

"We'll find them, I know. Mummy'll think of something," Jane said.

They presented themselves at the living-room door. Jane smiled a faint sad smile, and the traces of Max's tears still showed.

"Hullo. I mean, good morning," Jane said.

"Good morning, Jane and Max," Mr. Howson replied. Their father came in from the garden.

"Where are these famous soldiers, now?" he said. "I'm looking forward to seeing them again myself. Max monopolizes them in the attic, you know," he explained.

"Didn't you bring them down, Jane?" her mother asked. "What's the matter?"

"They're not there," Jane said.

"They've gone," sniffed Max.

The three adults stared at the children, trying to understand the meaning of the distress on their faces.

"You mean you've lost them? The whole bunch this time?" their father asked.

"They were there last night. We haven't lost them," Jane said. "They just aren't *there* now. Mummy, the window was open," Jane finished helplessly.

"Max," his father said, "you haven't hidden them, have you?" His wife had been telling him about

Max's deep attachment to the soldiers, and he wondered if Max was unwilling to show them to Mr. Howson, and whether poor Jane was shielding Max.

"No," Max said, "I haven't."

He looked at Mr. Howson, who understood the expression on his face and said quickly, "I'm sure he hasn't." He didn't smile.

"Jane, do you mean you think someone may have stolen them?" her mother asked.

"The window was open, you see. And you know the creeper comes right up," Jane said.

"Well, with this idea in the paper of their being worth five thousand pounds, it's quite possible, isn't it?" said Mr. Morley. "That someone would try to take them?"

"More than possible, I'm afraid. I thought of it at once," the parson said.

"But, Roderick, how could anyone know where they were? Anyway, it's a very high, dangerous climb up to that attic," Mrs. Morley remarked. "Have you looked up?"

"Things get around. Let's go and inspect," their father said at once.

They went out the back door and stood in a row, looking up at the open attic window and the vine.

"He'd have the pipe to help, part of the way," Mrs. Morley said.

"Look, if someone's been up the creeper there'll be broken vines and twigs," said Mr. Morley firmly, going to examine it. There wasn't a broken twig or crushed leaf or bruised patch of bark anywhere, as far as they could see. The paint on the pipe was unscratched.

As Max looked up he thought of Stumps, and an idea came into his head.

"It's more likely someone who has the run of the house," said the parson. "Perhaps?" he added, for this seemed a nasty thing to suggest.

"But no one sleeps in. I only have the daily maid, and there's Bill." Max's mother said.

"Bill helps me. He knows. He spoke of it. But I trust Bill."

Then Mrs. Morley said, "Oh, Jane, have you asked Philip? Philip may have taken them, borrowed them, put them safely somewhere ready for this professor! Have you heard, Mr. Howson, the American professor may be coming?"

"I did hear a rumor about it in the village. I was rather upset at the idea of their going to America."

"They're not going," Max said furiously. "Where's Philip? I'll *kill* him if he's taken them—"

"Max, Max don't be so violent. He can't hurt them," Mrs. Morley said.

At this minute Philip circled into the yard on his bicycle.

Max ran over and seized the handle bars.

"Where are the soldiers? Have you taken the soldiers?" he screamed angrily.

"Of course I haven't. Why should I?" Philip replied, also angry, because he knew that Max was hurt about what he had done. If you've injured another person, it's hard to be decent to him.

"How do you do, Mr. Howson," Philip added in his most grown-up manner.

"They've gone," Jane announced.

"Someone's stolen them for the five thousand," Philip said immediately.

Then everybody began explaining why this was so difficult.

"Look here," Mr. Morley said at last to Mr. Howson, "do you think I ought to tell the police? Just how valuable are they? *Are* they worth all that money? Are they historically interesting enough to be at Haworth? In other words, *are* they the Brontës' soldiers?"

"But I haven't seen them," said Mr. Howson. "It's an artificial value of course, but if there was proof, this man's willing to pay that much. That's what gives them value to the general public. If *I* thought they were Branwell's, I'd want to put them in the Haworth Museum," he finished. "Of course."

Mr. Morley looked at Philip.

"You've seen them lately, Phil, and read the description in the book. What do you think? Do I tell the police?"

"Ask Max," Philip said. "Max thinks they're the Brontë ones. Jane does, too, I guess."

"Do you, Max?"

Max looked cornered. He was bright enough to see what was coming. He looked at Jane, as if for help.

"Yes," he said at last.

"Why?" asked his father, and he sounded fiercer than he was, because he was puzzled.

152

"Just tell us why, Maxy," his mother said. But Max said nothing.

"Did you find something with them that gave you the idea?" she went on gently.

"No. You saw the piece of rag they were in."

"Have you found anything else in the attic to do with the Brontës?" his father asked.

"No," Max said dully.

"Well, what gave you the idea of calling them the Twelves? And those names, Butter and Stumps?" Philip asked, joining in the questioning.

"I can't explain," Max said.

"Do you know, Jane?"

"Yes, but I can't explain," she said.

Mr. Morley looked explosive, and probably only kept from blowing up because of the presence of the parson.

"We can't do anything to help you get them back unless you tell us all you know," he said. "I can't go to the police about any old wooden soldiers, Max. But I *can* go to them about the Brontë soldiers for which America will pay five thousand and which Haworth will soon be demanding. Do you see?"

Max saw.

"I don't want you to go to the police," he said.

In the pause which followed, an automobile was heard turning into the yard. It was the reporter. Max drew in his breath, but nobody else said anything.

The reporter got out of his car and walked over to the silent group of people. He walked rather timidly as he came nearer. Jane was sorry for the reporter. When he smiled as if he were happy and she knew he wasn't, she smiled back in sympathy.

"I'm sorry to intrude," he began, "but I wondered if the young man who found the Brontë soldiers had changed his mind."

Mr. Morley turned all his puzzled rage upon the poor reporter.

"I don't know where you heard that my son had found any soldiers," he said, "but there is no proof that the ones he found had anything to do with the Brontës. And there's no question of your seeing them. They have now disappeared."

"Disappeared?" the reporter echoed, smelling a good story. "Stolen? After all, five thousand pounds—"

"We don't think it likely. And I've no more to say. So will you please keep the thing out of the paper?"

But the reporter thought it more than likely, because it was a story.

"But where can they have gone if they haven't been stolen?" he asked.

"I don't doubt," said Mr. Morley with irony, "that they have climbed out of the window and walked off on their own. Good morning to you. Come on, Mr. Howson. Come and have some coffee. I'm more than sorry about all this." And he led the way to the house.

Max's eyes brightened at his father's remark, and his mouth curled up. Jane glanced at the reporter and blushed faintly. Mr. Rochester noticed both these things before he turned away with the Morleys, leaving the two younger children in the yard. The reporter gazed thoughtfully up at the house and the swinging attic window.

16

The Thoughtful Genie Maxii

"T*HAT'S* what it is, Janey!" Max said. "I thought of it at once when Daddy said that the creeper would be crushed and broken! *They* wouldn't crush it, they're too light! Stumps knows the way. He's done it as far as my room. And the attic window was open, and I stood Stumps on the sill when I talked to Philip. That would remind him. And, *Jane,* I've just thought! B. Crashey heard every word Philip said to me about the professor and America, because he was in my pocket! He wasn't frozen. I had my hand on him, and I could feel him move. He was listening, I'll bet!"

They had run into the garden to avoid the reporter, who was still in the yard. Now they sat on some bales of straw in the far end of the small barn.

"Wasn't it awful when Daddy *said* it? Did you see Mr. Rochester look at us? Do you mean, you think Butter knows they're in danger, and he's taken them to hide somewhere?" Jane asked.

"Yes. That's what I mean. You know about Butter having mysteries revealed to him that are hidden from the others," Max said.

"We may never find them again," Jane remarked sadly, "and I can't bear not to know what happens to them. I'd almost rather they went to America—"

"Oh *no!*" Max said. "They must stay here."

"Max, how could they reach the attic window sill?" Jane asked. "It's pretty high, you know."

"They'd swarm up my piece of string," Max said. "Don't you remember, there's a piece of it dangling from the window thing."

"The hinge, you call it. Let's go and see. The reporter's gone. I heard his car."

They ran, racing each other across the garden. It was like a detective game, and they felt they must follow up every clue. They reached the attic, red and breathless, and dived for the window.

"There isn't any string, Maxy!"

Max puffed and blew. "There certainly was," he said.

"You must have taken it off. How *could* they reach the sill? The stool is too far away and they can't move things," Jane said.

"I know they climbed up the string," Max said stubbornly. "It has to do with imagining what they would do. I told you about imagining how Stumps found Brutus' door, and he had. It was all true. I can't always do it, but I'm sure they went down the creeper. But I can't understand about the string. If I think hard tonight, I may be able to see what they did."

156

Jane looked at Max, interested.

"It's almost as if they do what you imagine for them, isn't it? It's almost as if you put the ideas into their heads. As if you were kind of . . . kind of . . . God to them. This is what Genie means, I suppose."

"It was when I wanted Stumps to climb the creeper. Because just as I was thinking it he did it. But this is the other way around, you see. They've done it. They've gone, and I've got to imagine where."

They both leaned from the high dormer window and stared into the thick vine.

"You know, they could still be hiding *in* it," Jane said.

"I'll bet they're not. Shall we search the yard and the garden, Jane?"

"Yes," she said, "let's, come on." She didn't argue about the string. Even if Max was wrong about it, she felt as he did that the Young Men would find a way and that this was the way they had gone.

They searched the yard and garden thoroughly. Max lay on his stomach, and shading his eyes, squinted under both the water barrels. A toad's eyes glinted sleepily back at him from one. Jane searched in the garage and in the old stable, behind a pile of harness. They divided off the garden, peering under the overgrown borders and straggling fruit bushes. (The house had been empty for a long time and the garden was neglected.) At any minute they expected to see a little group of bright-eyed trembling Twelves staring out in bold fear. Jane was careful not to be too wild and rough, for she could imagine how terrified they would be, and yet how determined to be brave, encouraged by the stouthearted surgeon, Cheeky. Max agreed.

"There are all kinds of good places," he said. There was a perfect underground palace beneath the laurel bush in the front garden—dry, roomy and completely hidden. There was a rock garden, also overgrown, with little caves where twelve young men could easily sit in secret. But they weren't there.

"Let's try the barn where the bales are," Jane suggested.

But the only occupant of the barn was Brutus, wedged in a good hole between two layers of bales. He yawned and began to purr.

"I hope they didn't meet Brutus," Max said.

"Brutus, where are the Twelves?" Jane asked. Brutus gave no answer.

Max found one of his skates near the big farm gate at the front. He put it on and used it as a scooter, remembering that he had left them there yesterday and wondering where the other was.

Mrs. Morley had noticed their search and was puzzled by it. As they came across the yard, not knowing where to look next but far from beaten, she called to them.

"What are you looking for, Maxy? You didn't play with the soldiers in the garden, did you?"

Max was thankful for the skate.

"I've lost one of my skates," he said.

"We thought the soldiers might have got into the garden, Mummy," added Jane truthfully.

"Only if you put them there," she said. "What do

you think has happened?" she went on, regarding her two children suspiciously.

"I still think they could have been stolen," Jane mumbled.

But Max clattered off on his one skate, in order to avoid discussing the matter. It was too tricky.

"Of course, Jane," he said, "they might have gone much farther. They may not be on the farm at all."

"I know. But which direction should we look?"

"We'll have to look in every direction if we want to find them. But I tell you what. They won't walk around in the daytime."

"No. They'll hide by day and walk by night if they're going anywhere," she agreed.

"The farther they go, the worse it is to find them," Max said, his eyes large. He felt that it was urgent to catch up with the Young Men at once. "If only I could imagine what's happened."

"Perhaps you can try tonight," Jane suggested. "It must be almost what people do who write stories, don't you think?"

"Well, that's what the Four Genii *did*!" Max replied.

In the afternoon they tried searching farther afield, almost to the edge of the moors. The heather was an endless hiding place for lizards, mice, grass snakes— or the Young Men.

When Max went to bed, he felt that they might be anywhere in that wiry, purple forest and that he might never see them again. But he would never, never forget them. He could imagine them all quite clearly, even their tiny faces, as if he only had to go

159

up to the attic and there they would be. He imagined what a bustle and excitement there must have been in the attic last night when they were getting ready to go.

He shut his eyes and he could see Butter Crashey now, holding up his arms to the others, saying, "Young men, a fearful, unknown danger awaits us if we stay here. We are likely to be transported to an entirely different, foreign clime. Uprooted from the moorland we know, which was beloved by our first Genii, we shall be put into a flying machine, helpless to resist, and not touch ground again until we have crossed thousands of miles of ocean. It is not that we cannot trust our present Genii [Max had to put this in, because he couldn't bear Butter Crashey to think he was treacherous], it is simply that they themselves may be powerless against bigger monsters. Prepare, Oh Young Men. Arm, Twelves, for we must flee!"

"As to arms," remarked the Duke rather cynically, "we have none. We must find them on the way. How are the mighty fallen and the weapons of war perished. Not a bayonet remains."

"There is a sack of glittering cannon balls," said Ross, "which, if we can carry with us, will not leave us entirely defenseless."

"Leave that to the ingenious Sneaky," said that character, capering about.

"I shall lead the expedition," Stumps announced, "because I have made this journey before the other way around. Now we shall go down the rigging instead of up it."

"Child's play," said Monkey, Tracky and Crackey,

160

skipping up and down, "especially to midshipmen."

"We shall see about that," remarked poor Gravey in his usual melancholy manner of looking on the darkest side, and remembering his narrow escape up knapsack hill.

The others remembered it, too, and laughed. Kings Parry and Sneaky were now standing with their arms on the sides of the canoe, pushing it gently back and forth.

"Think how it would help us across the great rivers!" Parry said.

"It is impossible, with all my ingenuity, to move it, however," said Sneaky. "Cannon balls, yes. The *Invincible*, no."

"Forward march! Leave everything," said Bravey, clapping his arms across his chest with excitement.

"Assemble here," called Cheeky, the surgeon. "You laggards! Stumps is already nearly at the top!"

Stumps was climbing the piece of string Max had left dangling from the window hinge. Max wasn't surprised to see this. He knew he hadn't moved the string.

"The thoughtful Genie Maxii," remarked the patriarch, "prepares for our every need. Up, Monkey, since you are so impatient."

Monkey swarmed up the string, followed quickly by Crackey and Tracky, singing "Way-yay and up she rises" as they climbed. Then followed Kings Sneaky and Ross.

"Now," called Sneaky. "The bag of cannon balls, boys."

Sneaky had dragged Max's bag of marbles to the

foot of the rope, by the string around its neck. The others tied it on. Then it was hauled up, clinking and swaying, and landed on the sill.

"Hooray," shrilled the Twelves, above and below, as the bag was untied and the rope lowered again.

Gravey attempted the climb and lost his grip only once.

When all the Young Men were peering down from the sill, looking like a frieze of figures in the moonlight, the patriarch was slung into a bosun's chair made by the midshipmen. It was really a simple loop tied at the end of the string. He held the colors over his knees, and was hauled up with dignified slowness, not because he couldn't climb, but because he was special. He was welcomed with a cheer. By now the sill was somewhat crowded with cannon balls, the flag and Twelves.

"Untie the rope," commanded the Duke. "Foolish to leave behind what the Genii thoughtfully provide."

Of course, Max thought, as he seemed to see the string untied and reeled tidily into a coil by willing hands. They took it with them.

They used it, he thought, even when they went down the steep creeper. He imagined he could see Stumps heading the crawling line, followed by five more all roped around. The rumbling bag of cannon in the middle was also tied on; then the remaining six behind. The six above held back the weight of the cannon and kept it from crushing the six in front.

How sensible and brave they are, Max thought, and he seemed to hear the rustling of the leaves as they made their descent. Now and then someone slipped and cried shrilly or another scrambled, clutched and swore. But on the whole it was done in an orderly way befitting the Twelves, even to the carrying of the colors. Once at the bottom, they untied themselves, the Duke told four strong men to drag the cannon balls, and they set off for the front gate in a line.

Here Max's imagining became a little muddled. It was almost as if he had been left behind and couldn't see. He thought he heard cries of delight and discovery and then many of their thin voices talking together, arguing. Perhaps they were arguing about which way to go.

Max heard Butter's voice, louder and more commanding, saying, "It is a carriage provided by the thoughtful Genii. It is ungrateful not to use it."

Sounds of hearty agreement greeted this remark. Then Max heard a familiar kind of rumble and saw the gleam of something that looked like a gun carriage. The Young Men had loaded their cannon balls onto it, and—six on each side—were pushing it toward the road. At the top of the slope Max saw them climb aboard themselves, the Duke giving a good heave and leaping on last, as a man does pushing off a boat. The small flag was held aloft in the middle. Then with a rumbling which grew fainter and fainter, Max thought he saw the little chariot loaded with their crouched forms disappear down the moonlit road toward the valley where the stream ran.

Max slept peacefully after this, without another thought.

It was only when he wakened in the morning that

The escape

he thought, It was the skate! It was my skate they
went on!

His mind had given him the answer while he slept.

17

War and Peace

MAX could hardly wait to tell Jane the clue of the skate, but she was down before him, having breakfast, and Mr. Morley was reading things from the newspaper again.

"Drat that reporter," he said. "Here's a headline: 'Lost, stolen or strayed? Strange disappearance of wooden soldiers.' I told him to keep it *out* of the paper."

"Yes, but, Dad, you have to be *nice* to them," explained Philip, "or they do it just to annoy you. You were pretty awful to him. What does it say?"

" 'What has happened to the set of old soldiers, possibly to be identified as those belonging to the Brontës, found in the attic of a farmhouse recently? They have disappeared dramatically, overnight. An American professor recently offered, in the columns of this paper, five thousand pounds for the Brontë soldiers.' The implication is obvious, isn't it?" Mr. Morley said, frowning.

"Everyone will think they're stolen." Jane said.

"And there are two more letters. One saying that there will always be wars while human nature is what it is, and why shouldn't boys play with soldiers? 'Boys will be boys,' it says, 'and girls will join them in such military games, whether they are Branwell Brontë and his sisters or the children who buy bright plastic soldiers today. Battle, struggle and adventure against enemies are part of the pattern of living, it seems, and much as we all now hate war, they look as if they will go on. Until men are perfect in humanity, they will fight.' "

This seemed a solemn letter and there was a pause.

"Mummy, do you think people ever will be perfect in humanity or whatever he said?" Jane asked.

"Well, do you think people could have been created with anything *less* to aim at?" her mother replied.

"But will it be *here* on earth?" Philip asked. "Or only afterward in heaven? Because I think it's dull if so. I don't know anything about heaven."

"As far as we can judge, looking at history," put in Mr. Morley, "there's no sign of its happening on earth now, is there?"

"Why not?" asked Max fiercely. It seemed a terrible failure on the part of humanity. Why didn't people do something about it?

"Because people *don't* love each other perfectly, which is what being perfect in humanity—put simply —could mean, I suppose," Mrs. Morley said. "As often as not, they hate each other and so they fight."

166

"But why does God *let* them hate each other?" demanded Max. Then he blushed, thinking of how he had hated and fought Philip.

"That," said his father, "is the deepest and most difficult mystery we ever have to face, and I don't know an answer to it. Mr. Howson will tell you it's because God gave us free will, and our will isn't all good, so we go wrong. Now listen, the other letter's very interesting. Shall I read it?"

"Yes," chorused the family, for it was a relief to return to the soldiers instead of thinking about such difficult mysteries.

"Sir [he read], the supposition that the finding of the actual wooden soldiers called the Twelves, loved by the Brontës, would add to our understanding of the famous family, is not so outrageous as your correspondent thinks. Let us quote what Charlotte Brontë says of them in her *History of the Year*, 1829: 'I will sketch out the origin of our plays more explicitly if I can. First, *Young Men*. Papa bought Branwell some wooden soldiers at Leeds. When Papa came home, it was night and we were in bed, so next morning Branwell came to our door with a box of soldiers. Emily and I jumped out of bed, and I snatched up one and exclaimed, "This is the Duke of Wellington! This shall be the Duke!" When I had said this Emily also took up one and said it should be hers. When Anne came down, she said one should be hers. Mine was the prettiest of the whole and the tallest and the most perfect in every part. Emily's was a grave-looking fellow, and we called him "Gravey." Anne's was a queer little thing, much like herself, and we called him "Waiting-boy"; Branwell chose his and called him "Buonapart." '

"Several things here are remarkable about the actual

167

soldiers. First, Charlotte's is the perfect hero, prettiest and tallest. Is this not exactly what we should expect of the young Charlotte Brontë, the hero-worshipper, who was later to portray Mr. Rochester, the most rugged, mysterious and perfect of romantic heroes, like no man that ever was? The Duke was Charlotte's first hero among the Twelves, until she invented descendants of his who took his place. And note that Emily's was a grave fellow. May he not reflect Emily's own character or what Charlotte and Branwell thought of it? We are told by Branwell in *The History of the Young Men* that 'Gravey's temper was still further soured by the sneers and laughter which the rest raised against him.' Could his grave face have suggested to Branwell's mind the character of the melancholy, reserved and overserious Emily? Is it an outrageous suggestion? In Branwell's story, Emily's soldier has changed to Parry. Had Emily, in the course of their games, gone on strike against being connected with the melancholy Gravey? Perhaps she had.

"Note too that Anne's was 'much like herself . . . a queer little thing.' As for Branwell, his first admiration was for Bonaparte. Bonaparte had straddled Europe like a giant, and to the small Branwell, already full of huge dreams, the very inflation of his evil success must have been fascinating. Bonaparte, to the average English child, was a bogey. Branwell could not help admiring him. The name of the soldier in question was later changed to Sneaky, which may have reflected the general feeling about Napoleon. Or did it partly reflect himself? As a character, Branwell tells us, 'Sneaky was ingenious, artful, deceitful but courageous.' Branwell must have known early how to use his wiles charmingly, to get his own way . . . Branwell shows a streak of comic realism, at times twistedly satirical, in all these young writings. For my part, I should welcome the chance to make the actual acquaintance of the Duke, of Sneaky, Gravey and Waiting Boy, probably the same soldier Branwell calls Trott, and later to become

Ross. As to the patriarch, Butter Crashey, who would not like to meet him, as it were, in the flesh?"

Max had listened, absorbed. All these soldiers were his friends. This writer, toward whom he felt great warmth, understood and thought of them as real. How he wished he could show them to him!

"And guess who it is? Mr. Howson!" said their father.

"Of *course*. It would be," said their mother.

"The brontyfan," said Philip, winking at Max.

18

The Gun Carriage

IT was certainly crowded on the gun carriage. The cannon balls took up most of the room.

As the Duke gave the last push and flung himself aboard into the backs and arms and legs of Gravey, Bravey and the midshipmen, he couldn't help sniffing. It was a little beneath his dignity to travel crammed upon a gun carriage with the common soldier (or sailor), and he wished he were astride his good charger Copenhagen. However, escape was the main object.

"Have the goodness to move those cannon balls and make room for my feet, Bravey," he said, clutching at Monkey to keep his balance. Bravey did so, pushing at Gravey, who heaved a deep and dismal sigh.

The wide road stretched downward before them, clearly lighted by the moon. They had set the gun carriage on the crown of the road at the top of the hill, and as the wheels rumbled gently and it gathered speed they could only trust in the Genii and hope that the road would take no sudden bends. So thought Stumps, who happened to be sitting in the front, holding onto the strap.

"I suppose you realize there is no means of steering this primitive vehicle?" Stumps said to King Sneaky, who sat next to him.

"Leave it to the ingenious Sneaky," said that small person, who had hold of the other side of the strap. He laughed one of his sinister laughs as he tugged on it. All that happened was that Stumps' end began to rush through his hands. He tugged it back, and in this way they continued for some distance, pulling back and forth furiously. The gun carriage kept going straight, quite unaffected.

"We can only go where the road takes us," said Butter Crashey, who stood behind them, his hand up to his eyes, gazing into the distance. "And at least we are set right in the middle."

"If the road turns, we shall be flung into a ditch and all lost," said Gravey, "but it is no more than one can expect."

The others jeered and Bravey dug him with his sharp elbow; his hands were busy holding the flag.

"We cannot eat and we cannot drink," he said, trying to hop up and down on the spot, "but at least we can be merry, old fellow. Tomorrow we die."

"And the next day we are made alive," added Cheeky, his red cheeks gleaming in the moonlight. "Take heart, lads."

"I can see the sea. I can see the sea! On the right! All silver with the moon!" squealed Crackey, who was squatting on the gun carriage and leaning out, holding onto Ross' legs. "Up the rigging and down the plank!" he yelled. Monkey and Tracky pushed their heads around, trying to see.

"Nonsense," said the Duke sternly, looking back. "We are coming to the end of it, and you don't come to the end of the sea so quickly."

"It's a lake, no doubt," Parry remarked.

"It's darkening ahead on the right," called Ross.

"We're coming to a forest," answered Stumps, who could see the trees.

The Twelves turned to gaze into the wood as the carriage rumbled steadily past it on the darkened road. Moonlight fell in flakes between the huge trees. Tracky seized Ross around the waist.

"Got you," he squeaked, feeling somewhat frightened, and he held on tightly. Tracky, after all, was only ten, and it was many years since he had faced the enormous outside world.

Now they were past the dark forest, and the road stretched silver again. But what was this brilliant and gleaming golden light in two great orbs, coming toward them so quickly that they could only gasp? With the blinding shafts of light came a loud and hideous rumble.

"The Genii!" said Stumps, shading his eyes.

"Monsters!" hissed Sneaky.

"Turn the carriage out of the road!" yelled Monkey.

"All is lost," groaned Gravey.

The Twelves could see nothing in the approaching

glare which came rapidly closer and closer up the hill toward them.

"Young Men, down!" ordered Butter Crashey. "Crouch, stoop, lower, bury your heads! It is the only chance!"

The Twelves obeyed instantly, hearing the patriarch's voice. The tall Duke had the greatest difficulty, but he somehow bent himself double. The midshipmen folded themselves away. Stumps and Sneaky leaned forward over the front, closing their eyes. Butter dropped on his knees. The light became unbearably dazzling to the watching Bravey (the only man to keep his eyes open), then there was an immense roar and total darkness enveloped them. The roar was deafening, the smell sickening, the heat of the tunnel fearful.

Suddenly they were out on the other side, the lights were gone, the noise grew less. The great truck climbed the hill, its gears whining and its driver unaware that he had narrowly missed squashing the Twelves and ending this tale in tragedy. Fortunately he hadn't seen them or he would have thought Rat! and swerved to catch it in the cruel way of bored drivers on long night journeys.

"Tug! Pull, Stumps! Prepare to tumble, Twelves!" yelled Sneaky. "I'm going to stop this carriage somehow. The road is too dangerous! Another monster like that, and we may be done for."

"Save your breath! One, two, three, pull!" said Stumps.

Together they heaved on the strap, lifted the front wheels, and succeeded in turning them a little toward the side of the road. The carriage rattled on until it came to the edge, where it overturned against a tuft of grass beside a rut, and flung off the Young Men, pale and breathless but unhurt, except for Crackey, who had bitten his tongue and said so.

"You've had worse to bear," said Parry. Butter Crashey was brushing himself off. The Duke nervously flicked dust from his cuffs. Bravey planted the colors and executed a _caper on the side of the road, shaking his fists at the memory of the truck. Only Cheeky the surgeon seemed unafraid and unmoved.

"It is evident," began the patriarch, and his voice trembled slightly, "that we must now leave the main road, even if it is the shortest way home. Another time, such a gigantic monster might well damage us."

"There's a crossroad here," called Stumps, who had hurried along the road to explore. "A much smaller road turns off to the left. Let us take that. It's a good steep hill and too narrow for a monster of the kind we've passed."

The Duke took command. Three on each side, the Young Men pulled the carriage along the edge of the road toward the corner. Monkey flung himself on it, lay on his back, and bicycled with his feet in the air as if he were going up the rigging feet first. His apelike face was still blank with fright, but the exercise made him feel better.

At the corner they stopped to consider. The main road veered right, down to the stream and the bridge. The way to the left went steeply downhill, only the Genii knew where.

"It's the exact opposite to our way home," said B.

Crashey, "but instinct will guide us. Who votes for a longer and safer journey and who for the dangers of the high road?" The gallant Cheeky and the four kings—Parry, Ross, Sneaky and Wellington—were for risking their lives on the direct road. But they were outnumbered by the others, who shouted them down.

They tugged the carriage to the middle of the side road and once more packed themselves on. But their troubles weren't over. Not only was the road fairly steep, so that they gathered speed quickly, it was also somewhat rutty, so that in their haste they overturned more than once. Added to this, the road took several slight bends, and many were the spills at the sides before the Twelves saw a row of cottages looming ahead. Here the path turned right once more and proceeded gently, always downward.

"I smell water," said Monkey.

"I can see a stream," said the Duke, looking ahead.

"It's getting light," said Bravey. "Eat, drink and be merry."

"We are coming to some huge, gaunt building," remarked Ross.

It was a ruined mill. The carriage slowed down as the path leveled out, and the Twelves dismounted (for the last time) in the most dignified manner possible. They gathered into a subdued group and gazed up in awe at the big ruined building towering above them in the increasing light of dawn.

"Since it is ruined, it will no doubt be deserted," said the Duke.

"And we can safely hide here today and march

again tonight," added Butter. Parry and Ross agreed, and Sneaky added only a mysterious laugh and shrugged his shoulders. Meanwhile the three midshipmen, all their fright forgotten, had scampered merrily off toward the river, sniffing the water. They found a useful footbridge, which they came back to report.

Gravey, Bravey, Cheeky and Stumps were dragging the gun carriage, loaded now with the cannon balls, the flag and the coil of rope, into the shelter of the ruins.

"Lend a hand, you idle fellows!" called Stumps to the midshipmen.

"Cut them open and let their blood," said Cheeky, whose duties as surgeon often led him to make such threats.

"Eat, drink, dance and be merry," sang Bravey.

Gravey attended to his task and sighed.

Inside the mill, in a safe corner where they could quickly hide behind some rubble if anyone were to come, the Twelves encamped for that day. There was plenty of water from the streams around the mill, and the ingenious Sneaky even found a large silver canteen to put it in. (It was a small empty pillbox which some untidy child had played with and thrown away.) With three men on each side, the filled canteen was carried to the camp corner, and they succeeded in drenching only Gravey as they put it down.

Gravey gave a melancholy howl and the rest laughed shrilly. As for food, they had to exist on grass and water cress, but as Cheeky said, what could be healthier?

"Rum and oysters," answered Bravey at once, licking his lips.

Before the golden rise of the sun, Butter Crashey and the Duke had made a trip to the bridge. The river flowed fast and eagerly in the early light, slapping up against the stones, curling around them with bubbles and foam. A large piece of wood was borne down from beyond the mill in midstream, floating evenly and steadily. They watched until it was out of sight.

"*That* is the way to travel!" said the Duke.

"Undoubtedly," said Butter Crashey. "For this river is going back the right way. We must find or make a raft. We shall be there ten times more quickly than by tramping along the edge, dragging that carriage."

They hurried back to the mill and gave the order to the Twelves to search for a boat or a raft big enough to carry them all, their cannon balls, the flag and their coil of rope, and for oars or paddles to steer it with.

"If only we had the *Invincible*!" Gravey sighed, as he went off to hunt with the rest.

"Trot along," said Ross. "No time to lose. Day is here." And he pinched Gravey to hurry him up.

Parry found the plank and called the rest to help carry it. It was launched on a side stream for a test, and found seaworthy. The others brought sticks for paddles. They hid the raft down by the stream near the footbridge, and all was ready before the first cottage door opened in the lane above them and the first twist of smoke went up into the frail blue sky. Then the Twelves climbed into their secret corner in the mill, ate their plain breakfast, and despite the persistent singing of Bravey joined by Sneaky and Stumps, fell asleep one by one.

Crackey was wakened at dusk by the fearful flapping of the wings of a pigeon coming in to roost. However, he stroked his crack to give himself courage, and woke the others without alarm. As soon as night came down they were on the move again, and long before moonrise they were huddled in a hole in the riverbank near their raft, waiting to embark.

"The moon rises late," said Ross. "Let us not wait for it."

The patriarch stuck his head out of the hole and gazed at the summer night. It was starry and not pitch dark. "We will embark at once," he said.

The Twelves cheered. A water rat behind the next birch tree, hearing a strange, shrill sound that he didn't recognize, dived into the river with a hollow *plop* and swam rapidly for the other shore.

The plank had one advantage. There was a nail hole at one end and a wide slot near the middle where another piece of wood had once been mortised to it. Monkey had passed their rope through the hole and tied the raft to a birch tree branch. They put the bag of cannon balls into the slot, to prevent its sliding around, and planted the flag on top. When everyone else had embarked, the patriarch stepped aboard, carrying his pole over his shoulder, and made his way up to the bow. The Duke, who was the tallest and could wield the longest pole, stood in the stern to steer, as if the raft were a punt. Then the midshipmen untied the painter and coiled the rope. The Duke

The raft

gave a great push at the bank with his pole, and the raft was off—away into midstream and gliding gaily along over the dark twisted water where the reflections of the stars danced.

At first nobody spoke. The Young Men waited, their hearts beating and their senses alert, for their raft to prove herself. Gravey, for one, expected to be flung into the cold water instantly. But as the vessel plied her way steadily and bravely downstream they took heart and a contented whispering arose among them.

The water rat saw and heard these things with astonishment from the other bank.

As their eyes grew used to the dark they could see the bushes and trees with arms stretched over the stream. When they heard a faster tumble of water ahead, Sneaky and Stumps would call out where the rocks lay and order the rowers on right or left to guide the raft past them by paddling. All went so well that soon the midshipmen, joined by Bravey and Stumps, were singing a cheerful song:

"We'll rant and we'll roar, all o'er the wild ocean,
We'll rant and we'll roar, all o'er the wild seas,
Until we strike soundings in the Channel of old England,
From Ushant to Scilly is thirty-five leagues."

The rat, swimming along curiously behind, kept a discreet distance as he listened.

When they had traveled what seemed to them several miles, the raft—carried swiftly by a particularly strong swirl of water around a bend in the

180

stream—hit against the underpart of a large stone (which Stumps and Sneaky, being more interested in the distance between Ushant and Scilly, had failed to notice) and turned turtle sideways, sliding all but a few cautious soldiers into the water. Stumps, right in the bow, got the impact of this terrific jolt first. He flew through the air, hit his head on a stone, and when he came to, found himself in midstream, floating he knew not where in total silence and darkness.

Butter Crashey was flung against the cannon balls, and clutched at them. The Duke, Bravey and Gravey, balanced on the up-side of the raft, kept their footing, and righted it. The water was full of screaming, swearing, chattering Twelves. The painter was hastily untied by Bravey and flung to the less fortunate floundering in the water. The bold Cheeky rescued Crackey, aged five, and nearly lost his own life in the process. Some scrambled onto the rock. The other two midshipmen swam, choking, to the shore. Gravey helped Ross and Parry aboard. The patriarch came to his senses and found he was embracing the cannon balls and the colors. He quickly gave the order to abandon ship for the moment, since all were too cold to sit cramped on deck. Dragging the bag of cannon balls between them, he, Ross and the others still aboard picked their dangerous way to shore by the shallow steppingstones at the side of the stream, leaping and sliding and cursing the cannon balls like true soldiers.

"It was Stumps' fault," Bravey said furiously, his usual good cheer gone. "Not to mention Sneaky. They

weren't looking where we were going." He angrily stuck the flag into the soft earth.

"We were! We were!" screamed Sneaky.

"Old Stumpy! Bandy legs! Bonehead!" Bravey went on rudely, jumping to warm himself.

"Blame none of the Twelves," said the patriarch. "Only be thankful we are saved."

"I blame Bonehead," Bravey repeated.

The young men looked around in the light of the now risen moon, expecting Stumps to answer for himself or to land Bravey a good right punch on the nose.

"Where *is* Stumps?" several asked together.

The Duke and Butter began to count the men.

"Stumps! Stumps, where are you?" some called beside the river.

"He is lost," groaned Gravey, "and has paid his penalty."

The situation was too solemn for anybody to laugh.

"Nonsense," said the Duke. "Not Stumps. We shall see him again as we always have."

"Duke of York, Frederic Guelph, Frederic the First, Frederic the Second!" called young Crackey at the edge of the river, slapping his chest with his arms to warm himself.

But of course, there was no answer, since Stumps was already several leagues away and was unfit for conversation anyway.

"We will search by day," said the patriarch. "Meanwhile let us march to warm ourselves, Wellesley."

"Certainly," said the Duke. He ordered six men to

pull the cannon balls and Gravey to carry the rope around his neck.

"And but a rope to hang himself," sang poor Gravey in the most quavering and melancholy of tones which caused delight to the midshipmen, in spite of the loss of Stumps.

They climbed up into the field and set out briskly downhill, the river running alongside.

19

Butter Crashey

"So what we've got to do, Janey," Max announced when he had told her everything, "is to find my skate. That will give us some idea of which way they've gone."

"Yes," she said. She was very impressed by Max's dream or imagining or vision about the Young Men's departure, and particularly about the string.

"And by the way, my marbles *have* disappeared," Max added.

This seemed to Jane even more amazing. She opened her great blue eyes and said "Goodness!" very gustily.

"Come on. Let's go," Max said, leaping up.

First they bicycled to the bottom of the hill which led out of their village, down the road upon which Max thought he had imagined the Twelves going. The road took a turn to the right and to a stream which they crossed by a bridge. Then the road began to climb again. All the way along, Jane and Max searched the edge of the road, one taking each side, for some trace, some faint clue of the missing soldiers.

But they found nothing, not a detail which might help them, much less Max's skate. Over the bridge when the road climbed again, Max jumped off and searched beside the road.

"I thought perhaps they might have left the skate here," he said forlornly. "After all, it would be heavy to pull uphill."

"Yes," Jane muttered. It seemed hopeless. The world was so immense; the Young Men were so small.

"If only it were *snowing*, there might be the chance of tracking footsteps. They would leave footmarks. Max, tiny weeny ones, smaller than birds—like mice perhaps," Jane went on, lost in her imagination. "Only not paws, shoes. In a column."

"Well, it's *not* snowing," Max said. It seemed useless to look for minute footmarks in the summer dust or even for marks of the skate wheels. There was nothing to see on the road, and as Max now pointed out, the Twelves couldn't use the skate except on the road. They must have a smooth surface or it wouldn't run.

Jane agreed.

"So where shall we go next? You know what I thought, Max, when you said this road? I thought they might be going back to Haworth. It's the direct road."

"So did I," Max admitted. (Both had thought it, but neither had said it.) "If not, they might go anywhere. Just to hide. Absolutely anywhere."

"Yes."

They looked gloomily over the bridge into the stream.

"We've got to try something," Max said at last, "so let's try the direct opposite to what we thought. Take that small side road where this road turned right."

"Yes," said Jane, who, like Max, thought taking the direct opposite was a kind of challenge to fate.

They bicycled back up the hill and took the steeper side lane down again. They passed some cottages, and following the lane, came out at a mill.

"Look, it's an old mill. It's partly ruined," Jane said, "and there's the river again."

"Not the same river," Max said, "I don't suppose."

The ground was wet and marshy all around the mill.

"You *might* make footprints here," Jane said. "Look, you've made some. Let's leave the bikes."

They did. They stepped gingerly around small puddles and shallow overflows of stream water fringed with grass.

"You see," Max said, in a dreamlike sort of tone which Jane recognized as the one he used when he was making things up in his imagination in their games. "You see, they camped here for the day. It's a super place to hide."

Jane said nothing. She only looked at the muddy ground for some confirmation of what Max was saying. She could see a little way into the old building where a door was broken. It was around by the mill-pond. She turned off the path and went that way. The ground was muddy between the pond and the door. Jane thought she saw a narrow, two-wheel track. She stooped down where it was clearest, and surely, surely those little marks beside it were the marks of their feet?

"Max!" she said sharply. "Look!"

Max looked and nodded. "Let's go in."

They pushed open the door, squeezed in, and looked around, blinking.

In the corner by a big pile of fallen stones Max's skate gleamed. They both exclaimed and rushed toward it and peeped behind the stones, as if the Young Men might still be there waiting!

There was only an old pillbox, half full of water, and a little pile of withered water cress.

"This is where they camped," Max said. "Look at their water!"

Jane nodded.

"And they didn't want the skate any more, so they weren't going downhill," she said.

"Or if they were, they weren't going on a road," Max added.

"No, so they must have been going over fields," Jane said.

"Let's go down to this river," Max said.

He picked up his skate and went out, holding it tenderly because it was a gun carriage that had carried the Twelves, and not merely a skate. Jane followed. They walked around the mill again and down to the stream and found the footbridge.

When Max saw the footbridge, he crossed it at once. Jane followed. Max was behaving rather as she had heard water diviners do, as if he were a sleepwalker. She saw no reason to stop him, since they had better look somewhere than nowhere.

The footbridge led to a footpath. Max marched along, an orchard on his left and a stone wall on his right, and the footpath led first beside the river and then away from it when the river took a bend, and then near it again, right along the edge.

As Jane looked into it she said, very quietly, "You know, Max, they could have gone by river."

"I know. This way, though," Max said. "It's flowing this way."

He scuffled along the footpath, thinking how much easier it would be for a Young Man to march here than on the grass, which would be tall to him. And then he saw the marble lying half hidden in the grass. Jane nearly fell over him as he bent to pounce on it. In the palm of his hand, he showed it to her.

"Recognize it?" he asked. "I would, anywhere." It was a particularly translucent shade of sea green and it had delicious wavy ripples in it, like flowing hair. Max had always privately called it the mermaid marble.

"So we're on the track," Jane said. "They've dropped it."

Max flung himself down on the grass and looked at the marble as if it were one of those crystal balls fortunetellers have, and could tell him things. Jane sat beside him, thinking and enjoying the sun and the noise of the water. The search for the Young Men made everything seem more magic. In every waving tuft of grass that the black-faced sheep had left un-eaten, under every large weed by the path, behind every boulder, beneath every prickly shrub or blue-berry bush, or swinging on a single fern frond strayed from the moors, there might be a Young Man. How comfortably Monkey and the midshipmen would climb that fern stalk, crawl out onto the spread of fern, and sit there sunning themselves! How conveniently they could lean—the whole lot of them—against that large mushroom in the grass!

Max started to his feet and raced across the field to the gap in the stone wall. He was gone so quickly that Jane, still lost in her dream about the mushroom, could hardly catch up with him. She managed to as he was climbing the stone step in the wall. Jane looked down at the glittering emerald moss at the bottom of the wall, and in the niche between the wall and the step she saw something move.

It seemed perfectly natural to her that Butter Crashey should be there. She had imagined them in so many secret places. Butter had stepped out of a hole where he was hiding, and now held his arms up to her imploringly, his face anxious and wrinkled for fear he wouldn't be seen.

"Max!" Jane whispered. "Look!" She nudged him.

As soon as the patriarch knew he had been seen he smiled and waved and bowed his head in relief and delight.

They slipped down onto the grass, and Max picked up Butter gently. Max said nothing, he was so pleased. Indeed, he had some difficulty in seeing Butter clearly because his eyes had filled with tears. He had longed so much to find him again and here he was. Butter pointed to the skate in Max's other hand, and rubbed his own small hands together.

"Waiting for us," Jane whispered.

"I hoped you would find the abandoned gun carriage, Oh Genie," said Butter Crashey, "and I stationed myself in the path, for I must needs consult you. The Twelves are on their way back home."

"Do you mean to Haworth?" Max asked.

"Yes," replied the patriarch. "When I heard the fate that was likely to befall us, I knew that only there would we be safe. There, where the four Genii used to be, we shall be welcomed and cherished and no harm will come to us. Is this not so?"

"Yes, it is," Max said. It was obvious.

"They'll never let you go once you get there," Jane said.

Butter nodded, satisfied. "So I supposed," he said. "It may take many days, and we have already had two disasters." He went on to tell them of the journey, why they had left the main road, and what had happened on the river. "And, sad to relate, Oh Genii, the noble Stumps is once more lost, for which reason I implore your help." He told them where they had last seen Stumps.

"He'll have floated downstream, Butter. We'll go and search for him," Max promised. "Where are the others?"

Butter Crashey stepped to the edge of Max's hand and pointed at the earth with his minute finger.

"Underground," he whispered, smiling. "In the early dawn we met an enormous monster, four-legged, brown, with whiskers. We opened fire at once. The

191

cannon balls flew fast and furiously. The creature received one on its chest and right paw and leaped into the air, all four feet from the ground. As we could tell by its alarmed expression, it was far more afraid of us than we were of it, and was about to dive into its hole when I implored it to stay."

"It was a rabbit," Jane said.

"You lost a cannon ball," Max said, holding it up.

Butter nodded. "It proved gentle in the extreme," he said. "Showed no wish to eat us, and led us into its domain. We have come miles in perfect safety led by this animal. I came up to watch for you, but the others are disporting themselves in an underground hall, singing merrily while Bravey plies them with underground water for wine. If we had but the noble Stumps, we should be happy indeed, having found the Genii."

Max had been thinking quickly. "We will search for Stumps. When will you march again?" he asked.

"Tonight," said Butter Crashey.

"We shall come and watch over you," Max said. "We will go now and work out the way and at the same time look for Stumps."

Butter bowed his thanks and smiled. Jane and Max smiled back gravely.

"Good-bye, noble Crashey," Max said, putting him down.

"Until tonight," said Jane.

The patriarch hurried along the wall, turned off at a knot of grass, and dived underground.

20

The Brave Old Duke of York

As Stumps floated along on his back, what had seemed the total silence of his faint changed to a gentle swirling jingle, the song of the river. And what had seemed total darkness became a bewildering pattern of black branches and moving leaves and moon fall and swinging stars. And the stars weren't those which had shot and exploded in his poor head when he banged it, but natural, friendly stars winking above him in the heavens.

Then Stumps knew that he was alive and had no need of even Cheeky's ministrations to make him so.

Huzzah! I'm not done for yet, he said to himself. But I had better see where I'm going.

He turned himself over on his front, and instead of floating helplessly—which his partly wooden constitution had made possible—he began to swim. He also began to sing "Lillabullero" in his well-known courageous way until a mouthful of foaming water put an end to the song and very nearly to Stumps.

He choked, coughed, and grabbed breathlessly at a black shape he thought was a stone, only to find it sleek and soft and moving.

It was that inquisitive rat. He had followed Stumps floating downstream, less afraid of him than of the eleven screaming Young Men in the water, and determined to find out what they were.

Stumps, being used to Africa, at once thought, Crocodile! Now I am done for! The shock brought him to his senses quickly and he struck out for a flat stone. The crocodile followed, but far from grabbing his leg as he scrambled up the stone, the creature—whiskers pointed forward and eyes shining—nosed at him gently.

"What are you?" the rat said at last, in some exasperation.

"I am Frederic Guelph, Duke of York, and sometime King of the Twelves, otherwise known as Stumps," said that Young Man, controlling the chattering of his teeth with difficulty. "And what are you?" he added, determined to give as good as he got.

"A water rat," said the other.

Stumps breathed more easily. "Where does this river go?"

"I only know the stretch down to the bridge below here, where it meets the other stream. I'm bound for there myself. You may have a ride, if you'd like to jump up."

This is an extremely polite animal, thought Stumps, and it is better to get to the bridge, where I can wait for the others, than to be stranded on a stone in midstream or hurtled along farther than I want to go. So he bowed and said he would be obliged, and mounted the rat's neck. He was borne down the river comfortably, able to look about him.

"Did you happen to notice what befell my companions?" he asked nonchalantly.

"I think they all got ashore," replied the rat.

"Excellent," said Stumps. "No more than I should expect."

"Are you foreigners in these parts?" asked the rat.

"On the contrary," Stumps replied. "We have been hereabouts for well over a hundred years. And our patriarch was in fact one hundred and forty when he began."

"I've never known anybody to start at a hundred and forty," the rat remarked, and became so involved in mental arithmetic that he barely noticed the bridge.

It loomed above Stumps, a wide and noble curve in the moonlight. The rat landed him on a stone where he could easily walk to the shore, and disappeared into a hole in the other bank. Stumps watched the happy water for a little, then found himself a hidden place on the bank and fell asleep.

It was high noon when he was wakened by voices. The sun shone through the arbor of leaves behind him and warmed his shoulders deliciously. The voices were familiar, and though monstrously loud, they weren't frightening to Stumps because he half recognized them.

"This should be the way, Janey," called Max. "I'll bet this road leads around to Haworth."

"Yes, you can see it does. It's miles for them to go,

but they'll cross this bridge. We'll go back and get our bikes in a minute and bicycle right around," Jane answered.

"Say, Jane, what a super place to play! Look at all these wonderful steppingstones. And there'll be tadpoles under the bridge. And boats! It's terrific for boats. I know, let's go and get the Ashanti canoe!"

It was the Genii. Stumps had scrambled to his feet, rubbing his eyes, quickly realizing that he must make himself obvious. *They* could rescue him. They could tell him where the others were. They, particularly Max, were his protectors.

Stumps parted the leaves, ran from his hole, scrambled down the bank and onto the first stone. The voices had stopped.

"Oh, Genii," he said, "here I am. Notice me!" He could hear footsteps above him on the bridge.

"Come on, we won't be long."

"All right. What a marvelous idea!"

Stumps clambered and leaped from stone to stone, his thin arms balancing him. Then he looked up at the bridge, waved his arms, danced and even tried a small, reedy shout. He heard only a commotion in the trees by the stream and the sound of running footsteps. Stumps stood gazing at the bridge and gulped. He was so small compared to them, they hadn't seen him. Perhaps they didn't even care.

But then Stumps pulled himself up. He was sure the Genie Max cared. What about the adventure of the creeper? He flicked away some tiny tears and said, "Come back, Genii. I am here."

196

Perhaps this was why Jane stopped, breathless, on the footpath when they were almost back at the mill.

"Max," she said in tones of horror. "We're supposed to be looking for Stumps. We've forgotten Stumps! How *could* we? We promised!"

Max turned scarlet and then white. "Help! It was that canoe idea. Shall I go back?"

"What about the bikes? We can't bring them this way over all these walls, can we?"

"No. We'll have to bike back home, get the canoe, and go around by the road the other way to the bridge. Come on, hurry! Poor Stumps. I've been looking in the river all the way along. I didn't forget for long," Max said guiltily.

Stumps sat down on his stone and waited for what seemed hours and hours. The sun had warmed the stone and made it very comfortable. He wondered where the others were and whether Crashey had sent out search parties yet. Would it be better if he followed this river back the way he had come, hoping to find them? This was what he would do if the Genii didn't return.

But the Genii did return. Stumps' heart leaped for joy as he heard their voices again. They jumped off their bicycles. The Genie Maxii came scrambling down the bank very near to him.

"I'm going to search every hole and every stone along this bank!" he shouted.

"I thought we were going to launch the canoe," said the Genie Janeii, following him.

"You can. I have to look for Stumps," Max said,

sounding worried and ashamed. "He could have been washed ashore anywhere."

Stumps almost laughed. They had even brought the *Invincible* to rescue him. He only had to attract their great attention and avoid the Genie Janeii's large, pink, bare feet as she tiptoed from stone to stone.

"It's floating beautifully. There's a frog on that stone. It's going to jump. See?"

"Where?" Max hurried across. Stumps waved his arms and shouted with all his might. "That's not a frog, that's Stumps!" shrieked Max. "Careful, Jane. Bring the boat alongside. He can get in. He'll like it! Oh, Stumps, where have you been?" Max whispered, stooping down.

Stumps flung himself lightly over the edge of the canoe, and turned to smile at them. He felt very relieved. So did they.

"I've had a good idea," Max said when Stumps had disported himself in the *Invincible*, making several journeys with the Genii in command. "We'll leave it down here. Ready. It may be useful. For tonight. And we'll find some sticks for paddles."

"We must hide it though. It's precious," Jane said.

They did this to their satisfaction, and then Max picked up Stumps. They hurried back along the footpath, and Stumps sang *"Marlbrook s'en va-ten guerre"* in a voice like a gnat's all the way, but the words jerked as Max moved. It reminded Jane of singing while her mother dried her hair when she was little.

When they reached the stone step and the burrow, they knelt down.

"Now, Stumps, Frederic First and Second," said Max, "announce yourself. The patriarch and the rest are hidden underground. Tell them to make their way to the bridge tonight. You can guide them."

Stumps nodded and marched boldly into the hole, calling in a loud voice, "Crashey! Crashey!"

The call grew fainter and fainter. Then Jane and Max, with their ears to the ground, thought they could hear a shrill, distant cheer as the Young Men welcomed Stumps. There was the sound of many voices chanting the old chant, "Stumps! Stumps! Here is Stumps!"

"That's all right," Max said.

That night they made careful plans. Jane looked up moonrise in her diary, borrowed an old alarm clock of Philip's and set it for half an hour beforehand.

The alarm clock woke Philip as well as Jane. Not only this, he had already wondered why Janey wanted to get up early and needed to be wakened on a summer morning. When he realized it was the middle of the night, he was suspicious. He sat up in bed and heard stealthy movements from Jane's room next door. Philip had already noticed that Max and Jane suddenly seemed far less worried and sad about the loss of the wooden soldiers than they had been. Added to this, when their father or mother spoke of the soldiers and wondered where they were and if they would ever hear of them again, Max and Jane looked what Philip called cagey. Trying very hard to appear innocent, they succeeded in looking self-conscious. He had already wondered if Max and Jane knew where the soldiers were and weren't telling.

Mr. Morley had been persuaded not to go to the police. Mrs. Morley had told Philip that he should cable the American professor that the soldiers were lost, and prevent a useless trip. Philip hated to do it and kept hoping that the soldiers would be found.

It was no wonder that Philip connected this strange nighttime behavior of Jane's with the disappearance of the soldiers.

He heard her tiptoe down and Max follow her.

He leaped out of bed and looked out of his window. His room, unlike Max's, faced the front. A half-moon lay floating on its back like an idle silver cradle, and the billows of lapping cloud seemed to make it rock. He heard Max and Jane bringing their bikes around from the yard. Wheeling them stealthily on the grass, they went out the front gate and set off down the hill. If he didn't hurry he would lose them. He flung on sneakers and a coat, sped downstairs, seized his own bike and followed.

Philip spun down the hill, feeling a tingling excitement. He could just see the bicycles' lights ahead in the distance as the road turned right. The moon spread a silver icing over the reservoir which Crackey had thought was the sea. The woods by the road were as dark as enchantment. He sped after Max and Jane.

Now they were crossing the bridge over the stream, and he could see the silvered water. This was the direct road to Haworth. Philip kept his distance; he would rather not be seen. Before they came to the houses of Haworth, they took a sharp downhill turn on the left. Now—if he was unlucky—they would see his light if they happened to look back along the main road.

Philip knew where this lane led. He had already thoroughly explored their new surroundings. It led through a farm gate and then along a stony track to the old packhorse bridge. He would have to be careful now or they would hear him on the stony lane behind them.

When he reached the bridge and saw their bicycles stacked, he decided to stay there. They must be coming back. He leaned over the bridge and gazed at the water. Then he saw the bicycle lights throwing small searching beams all around the other end of the bridge, down each bank, over the stones and the water, into the overhanging bushes and holes.

Max and Jane were searching for something. Philip heard them whisper (Always, at night, one seems to whisper. Why is that so?), and saw the bike lights going away over a fieldpath the other side of the bridge.

"I thought they'd be here already," Jane said.

"So did I," Max answered. "Watch where we walk, Jane. I think they'll keep to the footpath, don't you?"

When the two reached the stone wall and step and the rabbit hole and still hadn't met the Young Men, they were worried.

"We've missed them. We should have set an exact place."

"We said the bridge. It doesn't matter, as long as

they're safe. Only I'd like to see them over the stream."

"So would I."

They flashed their lights right and left.

"They'd come out if they were here," Jane said. "They'd see our lamps. Let's wait. They may have come a roundabout way." She sat down on the field-path not far from the bridge, and Max flopped beside her.

"Isn't it fun being out at night?" she said.

"I'd be afraid if you weren't here," Max admitted.

"So would I, a little, if you weren't," Jane said.

She lay back, looked at the moon, and suddenly sat up again, as if she had lain on a thistle.

"Maxy! Listen!" she said, putting her ear to the ground.

Beneath the cold grass they could hear the faint and distant strains of martial music. Their ears to the ground, they listened, hardly breathing. The sound became clearer and clearer until it was recognizable. Frail, insectlike singing; but singing—a marching song sung to a brisk measure. Now Max could hear the words, though still muffled:

> "Oh the brave old Duke of York,
>   He had ten thousand men;
>   He marched them up to the top of the hill,
>   And he marched them down again!"

Then the song emerged, clearly and quickly, like an underground river reaching the surface. Max and Jane stood up and looked about them. Just ahead, from another hole, came the column of the Young Men, two by two, singing lustily:

"And when they were up, they were up,
And when they were down, they were down,
And when they were only halfway up,
They were neither up nor down."

Crackey and Tracky, leading, clapped hands to the rhythm for several paces, having no drum; then Monkey and Cheeky; Gravey and Bravey with the flag; Parry and Ross and the cannon balls; Sneaky and Stumps; The Duke and the patriarch. Jane kept them in the beam of her light while Max turned away discreetly.

The sight was so enchanting that Max and Jane said nothing but watched the march of the Twelves from behind until they reached the road to the bridge.

"They'll expect us there if Stumps gave the message," Max whispered.

Jane nodded.

Max came up gently as the Twelves halted. He turned off his light and stooped down.

"It is I, the Genie, Oh Twelves," he whispered.

They cheered.

"Will you cross by land or by water?" Max said. "The canoe is moored at the edge."

The Twelves were tired after their long underground march, and they chose water. Moreover, despite their adventure last night, they had an irresistible tendency to choose water. They had never forgotten the *Invincible* and the journey to Africa.

203

Philip, cold on the bridge, at last saw Jane's bike light bright against the far bank and the flat stones. He saw Max crouching over the water. He thought he saw them launching the Ashanti canoe. He turned on his own strong light, shone it down on the water, and saw the strangest sight he had ever seen.

Caught in the beam, the canoe began to cross the black water, ferried by small, sensible, active wooden soldiers using poles and paddles of stick, shouting orders to each other, rounding the stones with care, and at last safely drawing toward the near bank.

Max and Jane stampeded past him on the bridge.

"Phil!" gasped Jane as she ran past. Philip felt sick to his stomach.

21

What Are Genii For?

"MAXY!" Jane whispered urgently, catching up with him, "did you see? Phil's followed us!"

"I know," said Max quietly. "I can't help it, we've got to get them safely ashore." He picked his way down the steep bank and was ready to grasp the bow of the canoe as it glided in. It was still held in the beam of Philip's flashlight. The patriarch held both arms in the air, and Max could see he was smiling.

"The Genii are everywhere," he said.

One by one the Young Men disembarked as Max held the boat, and they began climbing the bank of the river like General Wolfe's men up the Heights of Abraham. Some went on all fours, some clung to stalks and grasses, one suggested using the rope which still hung around Gravey's neck, but the others were too impatient to wait. Gravey himself stumbled more than once, lost his footing, and rolled back on the Duke. As for Ross, he was attempting to haul the bag of cannon balls, the others having forgotten them in their haste. Added to this, the beam of light was momentarily gone and the moon didn't reach the dark bank under the side of the bridge.

Max turned on his own light and relieved Ross of the marbles. Butter Crashey came last, as usual, in his alert and dignified manner, though even he had to scramble in places.

Jane was waiting at the top of the bank, shining her light to guide them. And Philip.

Philip was squatting down, holding his own light steady, as if to see better what he couldn't believe. He was perfectly quiet and rather pale. He watched the mountaineering of the Twelves with growing excitement, and the whole mystery of Max's behavior made itself clear as he watched. He felt sharp regret and jealousy that he hadn't known sooner. But Jane's gentle quietness as she had whispered, "Hullo!" prevented his bursting out with "Why didn't you tell me?" as he wanted to. He realized that his presence might frighten them; his voice would be unknown. Why hadn't he seen they were alive when he handled them in the attic? He supposed they feigned wooden when they chose. Philip wasn't stupid. He fitted the pieces neatly into the puzzle as he crouched there watching.

Now they were forming themselves into a column, two by two, on the road. This strange, squeaking, crackling noise! It must be their voices. Could Jane and Max understand what they said? If so, it only took practice. He strained his ears, concentrating.

Max scrambled up the bank last, saw Philip, took

206

in the look on his face and reached an immediate decision. He stooped down to the patriarch.

"The third Genie is here, Oh Patriarch," Max said clearly, picking Butter up. "Will you meet him?"

Butter Crashey blinked in the strong glare of the bicycle light and nodded.

Between his finger and thumb, Max held the small soldier out to Philip. "Gently," he whispered. "Butter Crashey."

Philip put out his hand, almost gingerly. Max placed Butter on it.

"This is the Genie Philippi," said Max.

Philip was reminded of the ghost of Julius Caesar, but he didn't smile. The little creature was speaking. Philip bent his head. Then, afraid of knocking him off, he dared to pick him up carefully and put him to his ear. The little figure was warm and soft. Alive.

"The Twelves welcome you," said Butter Crashey. And this time Philip made out the words. "I am their patriarch."

"I am proud to make your acquaintance, Oh Butter Crashey," said the Genie Philippi solemnly, taking Max's tone. Butter bowed and waved his arms and smiled. Jane loved to see him smile. Max sighed with relief. Philip, still looking as dazed as if he expected to wake up and find this a dream, handed the patriarch to him.

"Keep straight along this stony track, Butter Crashey, until you reach a farmyard. There you can camp tomorrow. We will find you a place." Max put the patriarch down, heard the Duke call attention, and saw the Twelves ready themselves.

The three Genii watched as the brave column once more set off along the rough sunken lane in the moonlight. Philip looked after them. What was it like? Like some loosely articulated lizard or huge version of a centipede? No, it was like nothing he had ever seen, that small column moving steadily, throwing its separate shadows, the little paper flag held above it.

"They're marching to Haworth," Max said at last.

"Yes," Philip said. And he sounded shy. Jane could understand this. He was confounded by what he saw.

"Will you write and stop that professor?" asked Max anxiously.

"Yes," said Philip, "tomorrow. Well, Monday."

"No one else knows," said Jane softly.

"I won't tell," said the Genie Philippi. "But what happens when they get there? Everyone will see, then."

"We don't know," said Max. "We can't imagine."

"And I don't know how to get them inside the museum without anyone's seeing. You see, they hate being picked up and organized. They like to do it themselves," Max explained.

"I haven't thought as far as that," Jane said, "what with first losing them all and then Stumps again."

"I'll help you think of a way," said the Genie Philippi. "Hadn't we better go after them?"

Weary and footsore, the slowly moving column of the Twelves tramped up the long hill, held in the three beams from the Genii's bicycle lights. The moon was often hidden behind clouds, and high walls hedged them in. Their way would have been dark indeed had the Genii not been like a pillar of fire behind them. Philip whispered, shivering. Max had the canoe balanced on his bike basket. Jane, feeling hungry herself, was worrying about the Twelves' hunger. The Twelves, like well-disciplined soldiers, sang to keep themselves going.

They reached the farmyard before dawn. Philip knew the layout. He led the Young Men to a straw-stack, where they could sleep warm and hidden between the balanced bales. The little cave of straw looked cosy and inviting as he shone his light on it.

The Twelves filed in, singing.

"Be careful tomorrow, Butter Crashey. Don't come out in the daylight without looking. People will be in the fields," Max whispered.

"I shall do all you say," replied the patriarch, and he disappeared into the straw.

The Genii bicycled home, cold, tired, and a little grumpy. They said hardly a word, Philip least of all. But their hunger was such that they raided the pantry. As they stood in the kitchen munching, Jane said in a whisper, "They'll be so *hungry*. I must take them something tomorrow."

"Oh, they'll forage," said Philip as he tiptoed off to bed. "Soldiers always do."

Philip was right. This was exactly what the Young Men decided they must do the next morning.

It was all very well at first as they flopped down comfortably in the warm, soft straw, so tired with the march that they thought of nothing but sleep. "Better than the captain's cabin," muttered Monkey, climbing up onto a bale of his own.

"The very best quarters and no mistake," said the

Duke. "Fodder for horses too." He yawned hugely.

"The elder Genie knows what he is about," remarked Sneaky. "He is as artful and ingenious as . . . as. . . ."

"The ingenious Sneaky," muttered Parry. "You make the Genii in your own image."

"Hush," growled Gravey. "Can we not sleep and be thankful?"

"Bless my liver and lights," said Bravey, "if that Gravey doesn't still whine! Give us good cheer, man!" He planted the flag in the straw and curled up beneath it.

Crackey and Tracky were already snoring, their young legs very tired. Ross had found himself a good nest and wouldn't bother to talk. The stouthearted Cheeky, leaning against Stumps, drew a long sigh of contentment which shuddered through Stumps like a wind in the rigging. Stumps moved up and curled into a ball on his own.

The patriarch surveyed what he could see of the noble Twelves by the light of the moon which now shone into the chink, but it was precious little. He could, however, *hear* them—snoring, sighing, grunting or muttering according to temperament—and, secure in the feeling that they were all safe, he fell asleep.

This was all very well.

But what of the sharp pangs of hunger which assailed them at daybreak? What was this that gnawed at Stumps as he sat up clasping his stomach? Crackey was already crawling around the cave, searching for grains left in the straw. But no grains

210

are left by a harvester. He found not a single one and was reduced to chewing a stalk.

"Hunger gnaws me vitals," said Bravey.

"Abstinence is all very fine," replied Cheeky the surgeon, now waking up, "but starvation is known to be bad for the system."

"Speeches, speeches," said Parry. "Let us go and forage."

"An army marches on its stomach," the Duke said wisely. "We must stoke up or we shall run down."

"Only a few green herbs in that animal's cellar," said Gravey dolefully.

"You were glad enough of them," Ross argued, jabbing him with a sharp elbow.

"I did not so much as have that," Stumps remarked stoically, "since you had eaten them all. I'm going outside."

"Stop, halt," said the patriarch, who had listened to these complaints (like those of the Israelites in the wilderness) with increasing anxiety. "I was particularly warned by the Genie Maxii to take care. Monsters will be about. I forbid any Young Man to go outside until I have reconnoitered. I may find food enough myself. Manna in the wilderness, who knows?" He looked around the cave, now lit by a pencil of sunlight that came through the crack.

"Empty me that cannon-ball bag, Ross," he ordered. (Max had decided to leave them their cannon.) Ross did so. Taking the sack over his shoulder, the patriarch stepped out cautiously. He blinked in the sunlight and looked around. He found he was facing a close-cropped green field on which a vast

211

number of immense white birds walked, pecking viciously and clucking in stupid pleasure. He could see they were birds, for they sometimes flapped their great wings. What were they pecking? If it was grain, then it suited his purpose exactly. He didn't want to invite a peck upon his rear portions from one of those sharp beaks, but he thought he could pick his way gently and not be seen. He saw no people, only the flock of chickens.

He eagerly set forward over the grass. Wide drifts of seed! Scattered bountifully on the earth! Like the manna for grumbling Israel! B. Crashey stooped at a convenient heap and with his tiny hands began to shovel seed into the mouth of his sack. He knelt to his task, for his back ached, one hundred and forty plus as he was. He moved on over the field, gathering the food for his men. Ahead was a building but it seemed deserted and it was far off. Daintily avoiding the fowls and dragging the increasingly heavy sack, Butter gleaned the seed, becoming careless in his zeal to collect more. The Twelves, who had come to the door of their refuge, watched with glee. Cheeky was begging the Duke to order a forage party to help drag the sack.

Suddenly from behind the chicken house bounced a huge black and white monster on all fours, and following him, a man. They strode toward the stooping Butter Crashey, the dog pretending to bounce at the chickens, who fled, squawking loudly.

The dog saw the small thing moving in the grass and pounced, sniffing. The farmer saw the bright cotton bag. Butter seized the sack and turned in each direction, tugging it with him. Then he felt the slobber of the animal and its hot breath and rough tongue, and at once feigned dead and kept still.

The dog snuffled. The farmer stooped down idly, curious about the bag. It wasn't a mouse, as he had thought. Whatever was it? A wooden soldier . . . Nay! He lifted Butter up and stared. Old-fashioned, well-made, a little shabby; not a bit like a new one. And a small cotton bag beside it, full of hens' corn. It was a caution! Or maybe something the children played with, left over from yesterday. Maybe it belonged to one of the children from the cottages.

He looked at Butter again and noted his high hat. What about all this talk of ancient wooden soldiers? There had been a piece about them in the paper. Hadn't he read that they'd all disappeared? Maybe this was one of them. If so, what had happened to the others? Perhaps he could get this news into tonight's paper.

He picked up the bag of corn. Only half full. Funny. He could have sworn he'd seen the little soldier move, cotton bag and all. I must be going crazy, he thought. But why had the dog pounced? Rover must have thought it was a mouse.

The horrified and hungry Twelves, watching from their stack, saw their patriarch stuffed ignominiously, head first, into the monster's pocket, and the food he had gathered so laboriously shaken out once more to the undeserving chickens. The bag was dropped, empty, on the ground.

As for the noble patriarch, he unfroze to find himself lying on his face in a dark, smelly, prickly hum-

213

mock along with a coil of rope, which he hoped wasn't an evil omen, a large pointed stake almost as big as himself, and what appeared to be a crumpled dirty sheet.

Butter made up his mind to do all he could to escape from these unattractive bedfellows, but he knew that for the moment he must stay frozen when the monster touched him.

At breakfast the farmer remembered the soldier, and, pulling him out of his pocket from among the string, the nail and the handkerchief, stood him on the table to show his family. Butter Crashey was passed from hand to hand, often head first or on his back, and he was dropped at least once. But he took it all patiently. He was also discussed as if he weren't there, and once more heard the tale of the five thousand pounds and the dreadful threat from America. His benign expression didn't alter, and was noticed by a small boy of about Max's age. More than ever, Crashey was glad that they had decided to march to Haworth, and more than ever he was determined to escape.

But when he found himself standing high up on a mantelpiece, far from his friends, hungry and assailed with memories of delicious chicken seed, only one thought was left to comfort him.

This was that the others would surely tell the Genii of his plight (he knew they had watched him from the stack; he had seen them). And if the chief Genie and the older Genie and the gentle Genie couldn't effect his rescue, then what were Genii for?

Butter sighed deeply and let himself freeze.

214

22

Wooden Soldiers Going to Haworth

THE Genie Philippi spent most of Sunday demanding a full and detailed account of the Young Men's doings from his brother and sister. All three of them were sleepy in the afternoon and they lay in the sun in the garden while Max and Jane talked and Philip kept asking questions and couldn't resist a few reproaches. "If only I'd seen that." He sighed. Or "I should have done this, given them that, or the next thing," he suggested, showing an ingenuity worthy of Sneaky himself. He got his mother's book and looked up all their names once more and made Max describe their characters and sayings.

How to drag themselves out of bed again that night they hardly knew, but like faithful Genii they did not falter in their duty. They presented themselves at the strawstack just after moonrise, wondering if the Twelves would have gone. They found a dejected eleven, still hopelessly waiting for their patriarch, and they heard the terrible tale of Butter

215

Crashey's capture. Added to the sorrow of losing him, was the Young Men's fear that without their oracle they wouldn't be able to get in touch with the Genii, so they cheered wanly at the sight of them.

Philip and Max at once decided that they must march and march quickly, in case the patriarch should be recognized for what he was—an antique soldier—and in case the fame of the Brontë soldiers should make the farmer search in his straw and around his land for the others. Meanwhile the thoughtful Jane fed them. She had brought crumbs and sugar and wild strawberries and milk, and the starving Twelves fell on these like locusts. (They had tried a few hasty rushes for chicken seed, but only after the greedy chickens had had most of it.) Bravey even began to sing "Canikin Clink" as he seized the acorn cup Jane had brought and took his turn at the milk. After discovering that it was a feeding rather than an intoxicating fluid, he made a face and swigged it down. Their spirits rose after the meal, and when they set out, several of the Twelves sported small, curled, white chicken feathers—like tiny ostrich plumes—in their hats.

The Genii oversaw their night's march, with the Duke in charge, and left them encamped near dawn in a field off the footpath, in the shelter of a rustling forest of oats. It was warm, hidden and would provide food. The Genii promised to do all they could to get back the noble patriarch. And Max, deciding that the loose cannon balls would hinder their progress, took charge of his marbles.

As they picked up their bikes again from the

nearest point on the road, Philip looked toward Haworth on the hill.

"They'll do it in another night," he said.

"That's what I thought," said Max.

"We'll have to get it done tomorrow."

"Poor *Butter*." Jane sighed as they spun along.

It had started to rain. This time they had had the foresight to put some food in their rooms, and, tumbling straight into bed, Max munched his under the covers, swept out the prickly crumbs, and fell asleep feeling happy in spite of the fate of poor Crashey. Why was this? Because of the Genie Philippi, whose added years and powers would help them to plan the last important part of the journey of the Young Men.

After breakfast the next day Philip went to the postoffice and sent the cable, as he had promised. It cost a good deal of his allowance and he did wonder whether the other Genii would share this expense and pay him back. Then he realized that it was his own fault, and stifled his meaner instincts under a necessary generosity.

WOODEN SOLDIERS GOING TO HAWORTH, he cabled Professor Seneca D. Brewer. There was plenty of time for it to reach him before he flew on the fifteenth. He wondered if he should say "Regret wooden soldiers . . ." or put Sorry on the end. But in the first place he didn't regret it. It was obvious that Haworth was their place. In the second, he couldn't afford an extra word. He would write the professor a letter, but of course he wouldn't tell him the real reason.

Philip bicycled home to the others, feeling relieved. It hadn't once occurred to him to regret the five thousand pounds which might have been Max's—the troop of living little men had become more important than money.

"If they had only told me earlier, the silly idiots, I'd have understood," he said for the hundredth time. He found the others waiting for him and reported what he had done.

"Thank goodness," Max said, glad that at least this threat was over. "But look, Phil. Look at what we've just found in the paper!"

Max pointed to a small paragraph which he and Jane had spotted tucked away in a corner on an unimportant page.

"Missing Soldier Found?" read Philip, looking at the heading. "Gosh," he put in. "He hasn't wasted much time!" He went on reading:

> "Walking over his land early on Sunday morning, a farmer near Haworth found a wooden soldier of early nineteenth-century design. He at once conjectured that this might be one of the soldiers, found recently at a nearby farm, which disappeared mysteriously from there one day last week. No report of their having been found has yet been received, but does this perhaps give a clue to their whereabouts? An American professor recently offered five thousand pounds for the set of soldiers once owned by the Brontës as children. The soldiers found at the farm were reported to be of the right period and design. Where are the rest of them hiding?"

Philip looked up at the others. If he had known how to gnash his teeth, he would have gnashed them.

"That'll be our reporter. This person who found Butter must have called up the paper! On Sunday

218

too! It's a good thing we made them march on, Max!"

"Yes. But what about Butter?" Max asked.

"You see, the five-thousand offer still stands, for all anyone knows. He's probably thinking of that, this farmer."

"Anyway, everyone around here's interested. Bill asked me the other day if we'd found them and I had to hedge," Jane said.

"If it gets out about the professor not coming," Philip said, "then everyone will know *we* know where they are."

The others looked at him, frowning.

"You see, I cabled 'Wooden soldiers going to Haworth.'" Philip added. There was silence.

"Well, never mind," Max said anxiously. "They'll be there tonight!"

Jane nodded. "Then they'll be safe. If only we can get Butter back!"

"Yes, and if we can get them *in* safely," Max said to Philip doubtfully, his face creased with thinking about this problem. "I think we'll just have to go and smuggle them in the next morning. Camp them in the garden when they arrive, and tell them to wait."

"No, I've got a better idea than that," Philip said. "Listen."

His plan was bold and desperate, but if it worked, the noble Young Men could reenter their original home with the kind of dignity which befitted them and completely—as Phil said—under their own steam. This was very important to Max, for he knew that part of their life depended on their being left to do things by themselves and not being interfered

219

with. He could oversee and suggest, but not dictate. And they had undertaken the whole march without consulting him.

"I wonder. I just wonder," Jane said, "if when they get there and the people find them and the visitors all come and stare at them, if they'll freeze."

"Not all the time," Max said. "Think of people's faces if they see them move!"

"You know, I'm afraid Jane may be right," Philip said cautiously.

Max's face went blank. "It'll be awful! I'll wish I'd never let them go," he said.

"Let them go?" echoed Jane. "You know you wouldn't stop them. You keep on about their having to do what they think! I'm sure it's right, whatever happens afterward."

Max nodded dolefully.

"Yes, only I'll miss them," he said.

Philip's plan also demanded that they visit the museum at Haworth to see the lay of the land. They arranged this immediately. Mrs. Morley was pleased to think they were eager enough to do this on their own, and gave them the money for admission.

"So much the better," Phil said as they jumped on their bicycles.

They had decided that there was nothing they could do about Butter Crashey right now. After all, they knew where he was. Later, perhaps they would go and ask for him.

As they entered the ivied gray stone parsonage each was thinking different thoughts. Max's mind was mainly on what his mother had told him about the

220

Chief Genie Branii, since he considered himself the chief of the present Genii. His mother had told him all she could remember about Branwell, how funny and gay and brave his early stories were (there were lots more besides *The History of the Young Men*) and how sad it was that when he grew up he disappointed everyone by never really using his talents. His nervous, excitable, feeling temperament and his oversheltered childhood had made it difficult for him ever to grow up at all. In some ways he never did. He had died when only thirty-one years old, not knowing about his famous sisters' success with their novels. But what Max was thinking of as he marched up the seven stone steps to the door was Charlotte's comic description of him:

> A low, slightly built man attired in a black coat and raven grey trousers, his hat placed nearly at the back of his head, revealing a bush of carroty hair so arranged that at the sides it projected almost like two spread hands, a pair of spectacles placed across a prominent Roman nose. . . . He had a black neckerchief and a little black cane flourished in his hand, and he walked with that indescribable swing always assumed by those who pride themselves on being good pedestrians.

It seemed to Max that he could almost imagine him bounding down the stone staircase to the hall, to get out upon some walk over the moors. Max wasn't at all surprised that Branwell had invented and made alive the adventurous swashbuckling Twelves—Stumps and Sneaky and the rest, the lovable Butter Crashey, the wild uproarious midshipmen.

221

But Jane was thinking of Charlotte and wondering which room she had sat in to write *Jane Eyre* and whether she thought of herself as Jane and if her husband Mr. Nicholls was at all like Mr. Rochester.

Philip was surveying the outside of the parsonage, its walls and windows, and deciding exactly how his plan was to be carried out.

They explored everywhere. Jane loved the kitchen with the bright copper pans, and was stricken silent to see Charlotte's dresses with their tiny, tiny waists. Philip went quickly around, seeing the layout of the house inside before he looked at any of the exhibits. And Max—when Max found, among the tiny books they had written in the minute, neat, black writing done to look like print, one which said *Second Series of the Young Men's Magazines*, he gasped and clutched Jane's arm, and together they whispered the title page.

"They even wrote magazines for them!" Max said.

"No wonder they talk so cleverly!" Jane answered.

"Janey, they really should be put with their magazines," suggested Max.

"We'll have to see what happens," she said.

But Philip decided that the nursery was the place —the little narrow front room at the head of the stairs that had later been the Genie Emmii's room. Here the children had played, the guide said, and written most of the little books. Here the Twelves would feel at home, if anywhere. Before the three Morleys left Haworth, they inspected on foot the last stage of the Young Men's journey. Then they bicycled back, their plans laid in detail.

As they ran into the house, the living room seemed to be full of people.

"Come in here a minute, children," called Mrs. Morley. They went in, wondering what was happening. Their father was there, and a man they didn't know. And Max's heart turned uncomfortably when he saw the reporter from the newspaper.

"Maxy," his mother said, "this is Mr. Kettlewell, and he thinks he may have found one of your soldiers. Apparently there's a piece in the paper about it."

"Yes, we saw it," Max said slowly. But what was he seeing now? What his gaze was fixed on was Butter, standing on the mantelpiece, martial and stately and wooden, surveying the living room with a fixed though benign patriarchal stare. Max walked toward him and held up his hand as if to take him, then decided against it.

"Do you recognize him? Is he one of yours?" asked the farmer.

Recognize him! Recognize Butter Crashey, patriarch of the Twelves! Max smiled. But he supposed that Butter must look very wooden to them.

"Yes, I do. Thank you," he said. "Thank you very much."

He and Jane and Philip all stood silently gazing at the patriarch, each thinking the same thing. What would happen if Crashey, recognizing the Genii's voices, should hold up his tiny arms and then bow and smile and speak to them?

"Mr. Kettlewell found him in a field on his farm, Max," his father said. "How did he get there? Where do you suppose the rest are?"

"I don't *exactly* know," Max said slowly, hedging.

"But it seems that people in the village are saying that you must know where they are. Our friend here, from the paper, has heard that the professor isn't coming and the soldiers are to be given to Haworth," Mr. Morley said.

"Have you stopped that professor, Philip?" asked his mother.

"Yes, Mrs. Morley, I have," Philip said.

"What did you tell him?" She went on, "That the soldiers were lost?"

This floored him. The Genie Philippi looked helplessly at Chief Genie Maxii, as if for guidance. The Genie Maxii stared back, his huge eyes larger than usual.

"I said they'd be going to Haworth," Philip admitted. "You see," he added quickly, clutching at a straw, "they will be, if they're ever found, won't they? It's obvious. It's what Max wants, and everyone wants—"

"Yes, if it can be proven they belonged to the Brontës," Mrs. Morley said.

"Do you or don't you know where they are, Max?" his father demanded.

"Not at this exact minute," Max said again.

"Well, Max, are they safe?" his mother asked. "They should be looked after. The sooner they're put into the museum's care the better. Is that what you've been doing this morning?" she finished.

"They're safe and they're going there," Max said stubbornly. "We can't explain any more."

"I certainly hope they're safe," the reporter said

"because everyone knows about this offer of five thousand pounds, and everyone who read today's paper knows that Mr. Kettlewell found one and that the whole world can come out here to see if they can pick them up. I think you've made the right decision, young man, but I've never known anyone so difficult to get a story out of. What happened?" he almost shouted, rising to his feet.

If the reporter had only known it, this was enough to put Mr. Morley on his son's side. Good for Max, why should he tell? his father thought. He punched Max playfully. He couldn't help being glad that Max was so hard to get a story out of; he was the same himself. Max half smiled and bit his lip as everyone laughed.

Mr. Kettlewell leaned forward. "I suppose this will make you smile, my lad," he said. "When I found that soldier [he pointed at B. Crashey], I could have taken an oath—aye, on the Bible if need be—that he was alive. I saw him move, I tell you, and the dog here did for sure. That soldier had a little cotton bag with him, full of hen corn, and it moved as if he was pulling on it. There! You see what your soldiers can do to a sober man!" He slapped his knee, threw back his head, and laughed. "See what comes of all this nonsense going on about the old Brontës!"

Max didn't laugh at all. He looked very grave until he Genie Philippi, almost too suddenly and loudly but really very cleverly, let out a hoot, hoping the other two would join in.

But the reporter stared fixedly at Max.

"He's not laughing," he said. "And he won't tell."

225

"Everybody'll know soon," Max stated, as if this were his last word. "And then you can put it in the paper."

"Bless the boy," said the exasperated newspaperman. "What's the good of that, when they *know*!"

23

The Chief Genie Brannii

BY Monday afternoon a strange and delightful rumor was spreading through the Morleys' village and the small town of Haworth itself—and even villages farther away. It centered upon Mr. Kettlewell's land, but its exciting possibilities seemed to touch the whole countryside with enchantment.

Monday morning, two little girls had wandered off to a field of oats near their cottage. Sitting down on the sunny green strip between oats and wall, rapt in some secret game, they had heard a rustle in the oats, as if a field mouse was coming through it. The stalks shook. The little girls lay on their stomachs and gazed into the silvery green-gold world of the oats, imagining themselves inside it. And at a short distance from the path they saw a column of little men threading their way through this forest in single file with a thin, cautious singing. One little girl later said that at times she could recognize the song and it was the nursery rhyme about the brave old Duke of York.

The troop of tiny men, dressed like soldiers—some with feathers in their hats—seemed so at home in the oats, the sun was so hot, and the green fieldpath was so silent and magic, that the little girls only nudged each other, exclaimed and admired, and lay watching, as if this was nothing more than anybody might expect in a field of oats on an August day.

They watched the soldiers return from their exercise. They saw three of the smallest of them swarm up stalks of swaying oats and throw down the ripe grains to those waiting below. They saw them sit in a stately ring in a small clearing and eat the grains. They even saw one, braver than the rest, come out onto the green path ahead of them and look each way and gaze up to the heavens, holding his tall hat. They kept very still, but he seemed to sense they were there, and marched quickly back on his stumpy legs. They heard a distant whisking, crackling noise like talk and laughter.

When the little girls finally ran home—the soldiers having disappeared among the oats—and told what they had seen, their fathers said it was a pity they hadn't taken the wooden soldiers. They had heard the story that Mr. Kettlewell had been telling about the one he had found, and it really beat all! Where there was one there were bound to be more. If these soldiers were the ones that had belonged to the Brontës, they were worth five thousand pounds, or so people said. Where were they now? Gone off into the field, the girls said. Gone off? And hidden themselves in the straw? Come now, no use pretending that wooden soldiers were real. They were just playing a game. But the children said they had seen them and heard them singing. The soldiers were different heights, too, not all the same. And yes, they wore tall hats like the one Mr. Kettlewell found. They said all this so seriously that it was difficult not to believe them.

Their fathers made excuses to take strolls along that field, and even lay down (when they hoped no one was looking) and gazed, feeling foolish, into the oats. Once down, they thought how possible it all sounded; the world of the nodding grain was so secret and reminded them of their boyhood. People in neighboring houses and people in the villages and from Haworth heard the story. Mr. Kettlewell's fields had a good sprinkling of visitors, tramping over their footpaths—some searching for their lost childhood, some thinking of five thousand pounds.

Stumps had warned the Twelves, and they went deep, deep into that field, and lay low; except the midshipmen, who now and then would swarm up a silver stalk and peep out over the whispering, pale gold sea.

What had happened was talked of in shops and postoffices and at the museum itself. It's strange how quickly a thing people want to believe gets around. This was a lovely thing—not only that the soldiers belonging to the Brontës should be found by that little boy, a newcomer, but that they should also be alive! Didn't it all fit in with the report of their disappearance? And where were they going? What were they doing in the oats?

At the museum, where the reporter spent some of the early afternoon, they said they had heard nothing about the Young Men coming to Haworth or even actually being found. They only hoped it was true, though they themselves doubted that toys of wood could survive.

Bill brought the news to the Morleys after he had been home to lunch. He told Mr. Morley what was being said. If it was right, hadn't Max better go and look for his soldiers in Mr. Kettlewell's field? Bill didn't see why someone else should get the five thousand pounds and he didn't see why the soldiers should be taken off to America if Max was against it.

This was kind of Bill. And alarming to the Genii. The last thing they wanted was this rumor getting around until both Butter and the rest of the company were safe at Haworth. They could only hope that the Twelves would be careful and that they wouldn't get lost in the oats and that the Genii would be able to find them that night and that all the people would have gone home to bed and not be hanging around.

But of course they said nothing of all this, and their guarded manner made Bill all the more certain that there was some mystery. What the mystery was he didn't know. But why shouldn't it be that this rumor was true? Bill went home again and then to the inn after tea, believing it was true. And since he was known to work for Mr. Morley, the people in the inn thought he should know, and they began to believe it too.

In the late afternoon that same day, Christopher Howson phoned Philip (as planned) and asked him, in very careful words, if he would like to come over and spend the night. Philip reported, also in very careful words, that he had been asked by Christopher to go and stay overnight. He didn't say he was going, but his mother assumed it, and so Philip avoided telling lies. It was very decent of Christopher to do this, because he hardly knew Philip and was dying to know where he was going that night, but Philip wouldn't tell him.

Philip bicycled off, with a secret supply of supper, in the direction of the Howsons' village, north of Haworth.

Max took Beurre Crashey (as the Young Men called him when they were in their Napoleonic mood) up to bed with him that night. When Max was safely in and settled down, he lifted Butter from the window sill and put him on the pillow, where he sat cross-legged in a hollow of his own near Max's ear, and they had a long and absorbing conversation. It was so close and comfortable that Butter didn't have to shout and Max didn't have to strain his ears. Max asked many questions about the Young Men and their life in Angria, and heard about the Twelves' town and about the great Glasstown, Verdopolis, which they built later. And he heard tales of Bravey's Inn and Stumps' Island and of battles and adventures and cannibals and heroes and heroines. He dared to ask, too, about their everyday life in the parsonage at Haworth, about the Genii Tallii, Emmii, and Annii. Last of all he asked about Chief Genie Brannii, and Butter laughed with glee and affection and said *what* a Genie he was! What a warm heart, bursting with love and admiration! Such artfulness and ingenuity, too, with which he endowed Sneaky! Such bravery and spirit with which he made Stumps! Such haughty

231

manners he had when he chose, like the Duke! Such comic mischief, like those midshipmen! Such bombast and boasting and exaggeration! Such tricks and spite, let it be confessed! Such a lift to the elbow, oh dear me, much like the hard-drinking Bravey. Emptying with the most perfect steadiness (I mean steadiness of supply and not steadiness of hand) glass after glass and bottle down his well-tried-in-those-matters throat!

And what about you, Butter, what did he give you? Max wanted to ask. There must have been something of him in you! You're so kind and dignified and calm and always able to arrange things, and you love the other Twelves. And the chief thing about you, Butter, is that they all love you. And so do I. There must have been something in the Genie Brannii that was like you.

But Max found it too hard to say all this, so he contented himself with thinking it.

After a pause, Butter broke out again. "What a Genie! What invention! The things he imagined for us to do, and the way he told them. Alas," he finished after a minute's silence, "how are the mighty fallen! Few people now read the adventures he wrote." And he brushed away a small, glistening tear.

They went on to talk of that night's march and the plan of the Genie Philippi. Butter was well pleased with it and rubbed his hands. Then, seeing that Max was sleepy, he lay down in his comfortable hollow and slept too.

Neither of them thought, until long afterward, that this was perhaps the last occasion they would have for such a good conversation—friends as they were—and what a kind chance it was that had brought Butter Crashey back to the Genie Maxii for that night.

Jane woke Max and they were soon spinning down the hill with Butter Crashey in Max's bike basket. They didn't approach Mr. Kettlewell's land by the lane and the gate (which led on down to the pack-horse bridge) but kept to the main road, and leaving their bikes, turned off down another footpath to reach the field of oats. They didn't want to pass the farmyard, in case any persistent people like that reporter were still lurking around in hopes of seeing the strange sight those little girls had seen.

But there was no one around.

The next problem was how to find the Twelves, hidden in this dense field of grain, restore their patriarch to them, and put them on the right road.

But as Max followed Jane along the path to the point where they had seen them enter the oats he thought that this was probably no problem at all, now that they had Butter. "Revere this man Crashey," the chief Genie Brannii had said, "because secrets one intrusts to him, others cannot know."

"Will you be able to find them and lead them out to the road, Oh patriarch?" Max said as Jane stopped.

"Undoubtedly," he said. Max put him down, and he paused a minute at the edge of the oats, looking both ways, taking a step here and a step there. At last, like a questing creature, he plunged off into the dark, whispering forest with a confident and determined step.

Max and Jane returned to the place where the footpath joined the road, and waited. They talked in whispers, Max telling Jane some of the tales Butter had recounted. They wondered how he would find the others, setting off into that forest with every stalk like every other stalk. Jane looked up at the vanishing piece of moon and hoped it would stay clear to guide the Twelves. Then Max had the idea of turning on his bike light and leaving it shining at the edge of the field. He went to get it from the edge of the road and at that moment he saw the car.

Max's heart jumped.

Somebody got out of the car and followed him back to Jane.

Max didn't like this at all. Jane stood up.

The man shone a flashlight at them and looked closely at Max.

"I think you can tell me where these wooden soldiers are, can't you?" he said, in an unpleasant tone of voice which tried to be friendly.

Max and Jane said nothing.

"You're the boy that found them, aren't you?" the man said to Max, and his voice was rougher. Max could see no use in denying it. He nodded. He was too frightened to speak.

"Well, what are you hanging around here for at this time of night? Where are they, eh? Hidden somewhere near here? Or is someone bringing them? I know there have been crazy rumors about this field. But there's no smoke without fire."

Max thought that they must say something simply to keep the man at bay. Jane came to the rescue.

"But what do you want them for?" she said innocently and softly.

"There's a man in America willing to give five thousand for them, they say. Come on, now. Where are they?"

He took hold of Max's shoulder and began to shake him.

Jane saw another car's lights in the distance, climbing the hill toward them. She waited, planning what she would do. It wasn't near enough yet, but it was the only chance.

"We don't exactly know," Max was saying in a voice quiet with fear.

"You must know. What else would you be lurking around here for?" the man growled. Jane darted into the middle of the road, held up both arms and waved them wildly, jumping up and down.

The car was stopped at once, gently, as though it must belong to a helpful person. Jane ran to the door, her face wild with fright. She could hear Max screaming suddenly. (His arm was being twisted.)

"Jane! Jane! What are you doing here?" said Mr. Rochester.

"Oh, do come!" Jane sobbed. "Quickly!" Mr. Howson jumped out immediately, but there was no longer any danger. The intruder had rushed for his own car, started the engine and roared off down the road, not waiting for anything.

"What is it? What on earth are you children doing

out here at this hour?" Mr. Howson said. "Max! What's the matter?"

Jane clung to Mr. Rochester, and Max took hold of his other arm. His face was shining with the tears from the arm-twisting he'd had.

"It was a man. Trying to make us tell him where the soldiers were," Max explained in a choky voice.

"Well, where are they?" asked Mr. Howson, naturally enough.

Jane and Max looked at each other across Mr. Rochester's stomach and nodded in agreement.

"They're coming," Max said.

"Through the oats," said Jane.

"They're marching to Haworth," said Max.

"This is the last night," Jane added, "and I thought they were going to get caught!"

Mr. Howson didn't know what to think. He stared at the children, then at the field of oats and then at the moon. He had been sitting with an old man of his parish, a friend of his who had been ill for weeks and had died tonight. That was why he was out on this road after two o'clock in the morning. Death was so solemn and made the watcher think such strange and mysterious thoughts about the nature of things, that Mr. Howson wasn't too surprised at finding Jane and Max and hearing a tale which seemed impossible.

"Coming?" he said questioningly as he squeezed both their arms.

Max bent down, shining his light on the ground.

"Yes. Here they are," he whispered.

In the light of the lamp, the Young Men filed out singly and silent, the midshipmen, Gravey, Bravey with the flag, Cheeky, Stumps, Sneaky, Parry, Ross, the Duke. And the patriarch last. They halted.

"So this was it. All the time," Mr. Howson said. He knelt down and looked at them. They weren't alarmed. They shuffled and stood at ease. The patriarch lifted up his arms to Max and smiled.

Max knelt beside Mr. Howson and picked up Butter Crashey.

"This is the Reverend Genie, Oh Patriarch," he said, and he handed Butter to Mr. Howson. Mr. Howson held B. Crashey up, and as he looked at him the moon sidled out again and showed the patriarch smiling and nodding.

"I have long wanted to make your acquaintance, Butter Crashey, patriarch and oracle of the Young Men," said Mr. Howson, who had been rereading all the Genie Brannii's stories since Max found the soldiers. There was a bright little cheer from the line of Twelves, all gazing up at the Reverend Genie.

"The Young Men welcome you. It was a Reverend Genie who first brought us to Haworth," explained Beurre Crashey, nodding his head.

Mr. Howson thought, I can't believe it, and yet here they are before my eyes. Such is the power of genii to make things alive. So do creative genii echo their Creator. He put Butter down.

He wanted to ask which were Sneaky and Gravey and Stumps; the Duke he could pick out at once by his height. But he decided that enough had been said and that he must no longer interrupt their march. Max shone his light at the road.

"Here you must cross a wide main road, Butter

Crashey, and there may be cars on it." He looked both ways anxiously. At the moment there was nothing and the lights of Mr. Howson's car lighted the road. "Can you hurry them across, perhaps?" he suggested.

The Duke had brought the men to the very edge where they stood ready.

"Young Men, at the double!" ordered Crashey. And the whole column bowed their heads, bent their elbows, picked up their heels and ran across the road like sprinters. Jane laughed with delight as each passed in the beam of the headlights; she had never seen them all run before.

"Splendid," said the Reverend Genie as they followed. "Utterly splendid."

The Twelves were panting visibly as Max stooped to see them gather on the other side. The midshipmen slapped their chests and gasped. Then they all formed into their usual double column and set off instinctively toward the footpath which led to Haworth and the parsonage museum.

Jane looked up at Mr. Howson and took his arm again.

"Will you come?" she pleaded. "In case . . . in case. . . ." What could go wrong now? They were nearly there. But there was the man in the car, who might think of waiting at the museum. Something might even go wrong with Philip's plan.

"Jane, I will most certainly come," said Mr. Rochester eagerly, "if I'm invited. I'm greatly honored," he said seriously. And she knew he meant it. "Besides," he went on, "I won't sleep happily in my bed until you are all—Young Men and Morleys—safe in yours."

He drove his car to the side of the road and locked it. He and Jane followed Max, whose light they could see ahead, serving as a pillar of fire (as Phil said) to the Twelves.

From her bicycle basket, Jane had brought a large, oval, hide-covered object which she carried under her arm. Mr. Howson stared at it curiously. It was the Ashanti drum.

"You see, we thought they deserved a kind of triumphal entry," Jane explained, "as there are only three—no, four Genii—to see them. This is the drum they used in our attic."

The Genii watched over the last stage of the journey, Max holding back the gates in the walls for the Young Men to file through. The others were near enough to thread their way past the stone pillars set in the wall. And near enough to hear the shrill cheer as the Twelves recognized their former home.

24

The Twelves Reach Home

PHILIP was stiff from keeping still, tired from keeping awake, and miserable from waiting. He was also faintly—just faintly—uneasy. As he leaned against the wall, sitting on the hard floor in the Brontës' nursery (which had later been the Genie Emmii's room), it was difficult not to feel that it was all rather ghostly. He had his bike light, but sometimes that made things worse as he flashed it around the walls. Anyway, he was afraid of someone's seeing the light. He had stationed himself behind the door so that he could hide if someone did hear a sound, come upstairs, and open it.

He couldn't keep absolutely still; it was more than flesh and blood could do. At first he had lingered in the little room, closing the door when he heard no more visitors' footsteps, and then simply praying that curators and others would assume it was empty. He stayed frozen behind the door for at least half an hour. This was good discipline and he was rather proud of it.

After that, as the evening wore on, he ate his food and prowled stealthily around, looking at things and peeping from the window. There was Emily, gazing rather timidly, in a visionary way (as if she were looking out over the moors), in the copy of Branwell's painting. Here were drawings the four Genii had scratched on the walls. On display were some of their pencil drawings too. As the daylight finally died away over the wild stretch of moors which he could see from the window, Philip found it difficult not to feel that the four Genii were really quite uncomfortably close. The whole thing would be nicer when it was over. It was good that he was in the secret at last, to perform this part. He thought Max would have disliked it, and he was sure that Jane would have refused point-blank.

Then he must have slept with his head on his knees, for he woke up cold and stiff. He looked at his watch. It was half-past three. He was delighted. Surely this vigil must be nearly over, and so far the plan had worked.

He crept over to the window, sat on the sill, and peered out. There were bike lights in the garden. They were here! Thank goodness. Then Philip's heart beat faster at seeing a tall adult figure beside Jane. This wasn't part of the plan. Who was this? Had the museum people wakened and seen them after all? He supposed there might be a fuss about his staying inside all night, but apart from that they were doing

241

no harm. Indeed they were conferring on Haworth a priceless gift (according to Seneca D. Brewer) and the fact that they had to do it this way must simply be accepted.

Philip undid the catch and pushed up the window very gently. Jane shone her light up to show she had seen him. Then he saw who was with her. Nobody said a word.

There was Max, shining his light on the foot of the creeper beside the dining-room window. There was Janey with that ridiculous drum, which was enough to wake all Haworth, let alone the museum people.

When the Duke, the patriarch, Sneaky, Parry and Ross and all the others realized how they could regain their home, they ran eagerly across the lawn from near Jane's feet, mountaineered up the grass bank, and gathered around the creeper.

"The great moment is at hand," said the patriarch. "Who will lead us?"

"Stumps," said several voices. They were remembering how Stumps had climbed the other creeper.

"I suggest the Duke," said Ross, "the noblest first."

The Duke demurred and suggested Ross. Parry and Sneaky, also kings of the Ashanti, were jealous of this, and Sneaky showed it by his jeering laugh.

"Not I," said Cheeky, "lest any man slip, fall, and need to be made alive."

"That is an encouragement before our dangerous climb," said Gravey in a mournful tone.

The midshipmen laughed.

"Come along, come along, eat, drink and be merry!" called Bravey, dancing a fandango on the top of the bank and nearly rolling down it. "Show your metal, men."

Oh goodness me, thought Max, if only they wouldn't argue now.

"Let the midshipmen go. Let the young rascals climb the rigging," said Stumps, who had been one of them in the very beginning, "and I will follow them."

Like Max, Jane was tired of waiting. She was afraid that their lights and commotion would waken someone. She put the drum down on the ground, knelt by it, and began to beat a very soft but rapid tattoo.

This was enough for Monkey. He let out a shrill cry.

"Up the rigging and down the plank!" He dived into the rustling creeper and led the way. He was followed quickly by Crackey and Tracky jostling for place. Stumps, the hero of so many escapes and adventures, went after them. Max couldn't help starting forward to whisper to him. *"Au revoir,"* said Stumps smiling, and he began to sing in his eager light voice:

> "Marlbrook *s'en va-t-en guerre*
> Marlbrook *s'en va-t-en guerre*
> Marlbrook *s'en va-t-en guerre*
> *Il ne sait quand reviendra."*

The rest took up the air as they climbed, and crawled and swung and panted, moving first up and then along toward the open window and the light of Philip's flashlight. But some knew the English words

243

better than the French version and they sang lustily and very suitably:

> "We won't go home till morning
> We won't go home till morning
> We won't go home till morning
> And a-hunting we will go."

The sound Philip heard as he leaned out was as confused, merry and spirited as sparrows in the eaves.

Max and Jane knelt by the creeper, watching each Young Man start his climb in turn. Jane picked up Gravey, removed his coil of string, and wished him good-bye. Gravey smiled before he set off. Mr. Howson, dumb with surprise and delight, stood peering through a gap in the leaves to see them pass, and trying to make out the song. He hadn't had much time to get used to their voices.

As the patriarch, last by right, prepared to follow the others, he turned to Max, held up his arms in the familiar gesture, smiled and bowed.

"Good-bye, Oh Butter Crashey," Max said, very subdued. "I shall come and visit you."

"Good-bye, Genie Maxii," said the patriarch. "You will always find me at home."

Then he turned around, plunged gladly into the creeper and started to climb. Max sniffed.

They could hear when Butter's slow and stately climb was over, for a reverential cheer went up from the window sill. Jane stopped beating her drum. The Genie Philippi had helped those who needed help, grasping them gently as their heads appeared, and lifting them to safety. As Butter arrived he put him with the rest, drew in his head, and quietly closed the window and fastened the catch. Gray curtains of light in the sky promised the dawn.

"Welcome home, Young Men. The place awaits you," Philip said formally, stooping to peer at them arrayed on the sill.

The Twelves were surveying the nursery with shrill cries of delight. It was clear that they recognized it and were pleased to be there.

Philip tiptoed down the stairs and let himself out the front door.

And so—their last journey over—the twelve adventurers returned to their ancestral home.

25

Night Life

IN the morning the troop of wooden soldiers, twelve in number and of a design like that described by Branwell Brontë in *The History of the Young Men*, were found on the window sill of the nursery at the museum. Beside them was stuck a little blue paper flag from a recent flag day.

They stood in proud, martial order, two by two in their usual manner: Crackey and Tracky, Monkey and Cheeky, Bravey and Gravey, Sneaky and Stumps, Parry and Ross, the Duke of Wellington and the patriarch Crashey. But the visitor who found them, snatching one up with an exclamation, didn't know which it was he grasped or the names of the others. How are the mighty fallen!

Everyone in authority came to see, as well as the early visitors. The window was closed, bolted and undamaged. The house wall and creeper showed no signs of having been climbed. How had they got here?

Someone had brought them yesterday, no doubt, and left them just before closing time, and here they were. It was odd that whoever had found them had said nothing about it. Perhaps they had thought it best to keep quiet because of the offer of five thousand pounds from the American professor. And perhaps the small boy from the farm in the neighboring village knew all about it.

The museum director phoned the Morleys to ask if this set of soldiers which had appeared overnight in the museum was the one Max had found in the Morleys' attic—the one that had vanished mysteriously. Mr. Morley said yes, these were the soldiers, and his son was glad they had reached the museum, which was certainly their home.

Now this was all very well, and they thanked Max kindly, but was he sure of the identity of the Twelves? Were these indeed the soldiers beloved by the Brontës, written about by Branwell and Charlotte, the originators of so many games and so many stories? And if he was sure, how was he sure?

They called the newspaper to report the arrival of the twelve soldiers at Haworth in a mysterious way overnight. That morning the newspaper had only printed a small, inconspicuous paragraph describing a delightful rumor which had sped around the Brontë neighborhood after two small girls were said to have seen a troop of little live soldiers in a field of oats. The newspaper didn't deny the truth of this, it simply described it, and the reporter had mentioned again what Mr. Kettlewell found and thought he saw, and the odd behavior of the young boy who first found the soldiers.

Now these same soldiers had reached their destination under mysterious circumstances. People could think what they liked about it. Supposing, the reporter said next day, the little men had marched back home? (Perhaps this is what he wanted to think himself.)

Visitors in even greater numbers than usual flocked to the museum to see the Twelves. The Young Men now stood grouped around their tiny magazines. A few people who had read the stories would say: "Oh *that* must be the Duke! And this must be Butter Crashey, the patriarch, one hundred and forty!" But most, who hadn't, looked at them with curiosity and pleasure, in case they were the beloved of the young Brontës. Nevertheless, they thought they looked very like any other wooden soldiers, and asked again how anyone could be sure?

How had they been saved from destruction and collected together in the first place when Branwell reported all but a few had perished? To this there seemed to be no answer. And how had they reached the attic at the Morley's farm? Again, nobody knew, and one theory was as good as another. Max couldn't help them. The Young Men had remained resolutely dumb about this part in their varied history. (But this was no more than Branwell had always said they sometimes did when questioned about their past.) It was evidently in their makeup, as it was in Max's and Mr. Morley's, to be wooden sometimes. And neither could Mr. or Mrs. Morley help on these pressing points. All they knew was that the Twelves had been found in their attic, played with by their son, and had disappeared from their house after the professor wrote to the newspaper. They admitted there was some mystery as to how the soldiers had reached the parsonage museum. Three nights running, Mrs. Morley, a light sleeper, had thought she heard movements, had thought her children were up to some nocturnal caper, and had noticed both their yawns in the daytime and the absence of food from her pantry. Mr. Morley knew that Max and Jane and Phil weren't telling all they knew, but he wasn't going to press them. And Mrs. Morley kept to herself (and Max) the strange noises she had once heard in the attic and the movement seen out of the corner of her eye, because both the sound and the movement had stopped so suddenly that she thought she must have been mistaken. But now, she wondered, what with the farmer and the little girls and Max himself . . . When Max said it was true, she could only be sad that she hadn't seen more of it.

So, by and large, the Morleys were no help.

Then the experts and the authorities got in touch with that nearby brontyfan, the Reverend Mr. Howson, who seemed well versed in Branwell's stories and who was himself a member of the Brontë Society and wrote papers about them and addressed meetings and one thing and another.

Mr. Howson visited the museum with the young Morleys after hours, when they could have the Young Men to themselves in the nursery. He came out of that delightful encounter absolutely convinced, from his conversation with Butter, that these were the Twelves (which he of course had never doubted) and moreover that the Duke was the Duke; and which one was Stumps, and which the kings, Sneaky and Parry and Ross; and which poor Gravey, and cheerful Bravey, and Cheeky the surgeon, and Monkey and Crackey and Tracky. Indeed, he was able to tell the authorities which was which, and although he had better means of knowing, he could point to Crackey's crack and Stumps' stumpy legs and Gravey's sardonic face—which was all other people could understand. This he did, and because he was so sure and was a grownup and a parson and a brontyfan, his word was taken. No one any longer doubted that these were the Young Men. As to Seneca D. Brewer, who flew over to see them, he found no reason to doubt anything; he would much rather believe. He took color photographs of them arranged around their magazines and invited Phil to America.

But what about Butter Crashey and the noble Twelves? Were they doomed to perpetual frozendom, now that they were on display in their ancestral mansion? What a dull and gloomy life for such characters; well might Gravey moan and Stumps kick over the traces. No! They kept their faculties as sharp as ever and indulged in night life. What they were up to at night was nobody's business, and only occasionally were they unable to get back again to where they were supposed to be, such was the boldness of Cheeky and Stumps and the cleverness of Sneaky. (Once, however, they were found in the kitchen, and it was thought to be somebody's joke.)

250

In the daytime they rarely, rarely show themselves for what they are. Very occasionally some child or childhearted person catches sight of Butter Crashey with his arms upheld (Max never knew if this was to make himself taller, or if it was simply to say Lift me up), or Bravey with his elbow raised as if to drink, or Monkey executing a few steps of an incredibly quick dance, or the Duke yawning or Stumps singing or Sneaky striking some attitude or Gravey groaning. When that person calls someone else to see, ten to one they are unlucky and the Twelves simply stare from their blurred wooden faces, all looking very much alike.

But when Max goes and is lucky enough to find the room empty and picks up B. Crashey and says gently, "It is the Genie Maxii," then Butter wriggles, warm and taut as a lizard in Max's fingers, and Max sees their blurred wooden faces delightfully change into bright living ones, each different and all eager.

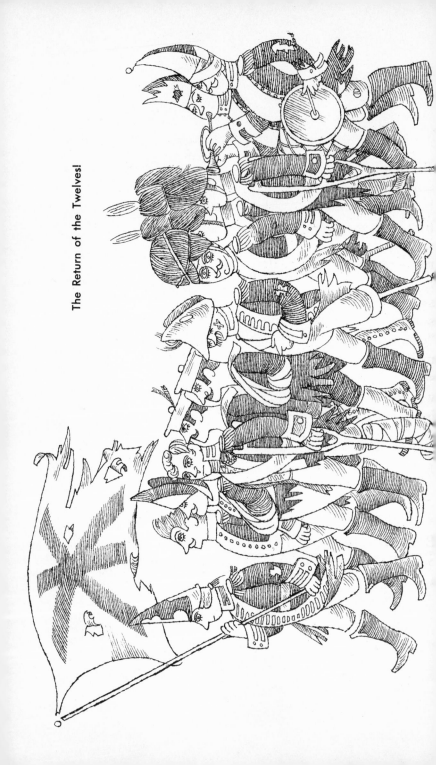

The Return of the Twelves!

About the Author

PAULINE CLARKE lives in an old and remote stone cottage at Blakeney in Norfolk, England. Her breadth of interests — language, folklore, history, literature, nature — and her instinctive understanding of the magic of childhood give body and basic reality to her works of fantasy. She has a knack of melting even the shyest of six-year-olds and of seeing in the children, places and incidents which surround her starting points for her stories. Not a "doll-obsessed child herself," dolls form the basis of many of her fantasy stories, and it is a set of wooden soldiers, the famous Twelve immortalized by Branwell Brontë in his *History of the Young Men,* which is the focal point for *The Return of the Twelves.*

About the Artist

BERNARDA BRYSON is an outstanding American artist. She illustrated the book which was runner-up for the 1962 Caldecott award.